To An

Hope to only for the young at heart!

Joy Emery.

THE CHILDREN FROM UNDER THE ICE

AND SANTA'S PRESENT

Joy Emery

authorHOUSE®

AuthorHouse™ UK Ltd.
500 Avebury Boulevard
Central Milton Keynes, MK9 2BE
www.authorhouse.co.uk
Phone: 08001974150

This novel is entirely a work of fiction. The names, characters and incidents portrayed in it are the work of the author's imagination. Any resemblance to actual persons, living or dead, events or localities is entirely coincidental.

First published by AuthorHouse 05/23/2011

ISBN: 978-1-4567-8022-7 (sc)
ISBN: 978-1-4567-8023-4 (e)

With love to my wonderful grandchildren,
the fundamental inspiration for the
creation and publication of the children's
adventures within this book.

PREFACE

Viridis 6000 dived from the sky and cut deep down through the icy waters at the North Pole and remained submerged in the Arctic Ocean covered with ice.

The visitors were no strangers to Earth. They had been before on many occasions to check on the health status of particular types of animals, which their ancestors had transferred to Planet Earth when they knew their planet's climate was changing and losing its rich vegetation that the animals required for good health.

Over the years, as Planet Viridis began to heat up and dry out, the Viriddions' had to make their place of living under the ground in special oxygenated thermo space ships, that could leave the planet, if necessary, to travel to other healthier planets, as conditions deteriorated.

The years continued to pass and many ships had left to other destinations. However, it had been decided that a University Control ship would remain, gathering data from all of the ships, for as long as Viridis remained.

Viridis 6000 had been one of the last ships to leave. Captain Genesis and his crew had been fully informed about the possible risk of not being able to return to their home planet. Planet Earth was not now easy to visit because over the past fifty years technology had increased on Earth and the satellites that circled the globe made it very difficult to visit without being detected.

None the less, Viridis 6000 left its dying planet and sped through the heavens towards the Earth with adults and children on board and with very specific monitoring equipment and machinery.

However, during the journey an illness had affected them causing death to many of the adults. As a result, the children are forced to make plans as to how they are going to carry on with the work their parents and grandparents had planned many years before them.

ONE

THE LANDING

Captain Genesis gave a sigh of relief, as he always did, when his ship successfully landed after a long mission.

He knew this mission would be far more difficult to undertake than the previous one his Grandfather had last taken. After all, planet Earth was now far more populated and technically developed than it was those many years ago.

The Viriddion Council had warned the family and crew that the return to Viridis may be totally impossible and therefore the purpose of visiting would be lost. But, Captain Genesis had argued that the visit had to be carried out. He argued that the ship and its families would have to leave Viridis sooner, rather than later, and that Viriddions' would never shirk from their responsibility to check on the health of various types of animals placed on Earth.

Sadly, though, a lot had happened since the ship had left Viridis and after ordering the crew to settle the ship and do the usual docking checks, he retired to reflect upon that journey so that his memory log could be recorded.

As Captain Genesis rested back on his lounger, he ached all over and he knew he was over-tired but, he trusted the Visionars recording system to do the job in hand, without any effort from him. But, although he knew they were designed to have therapeutic qualities for times like these, he wasn't looking forward to reliving the past months. Nevertheless, in a disciplinary fashion he placed the Visionars across his eyes.

The Visionars, an anagram for <u>V</u>iriddion <u>I</u>ntense <u>S</u>ensory <u>I</u>nsight and <u>O</u>cular <u>N</u>euron <u>R</u>ay <u>S</u>pectacles, had an amazing ability to read a persons thoughts and if instructed could record them directly to the ships log.

So...as Captain Genesis began to reflect, so did the Visionars record......?

Planet Viridis Status: ... Ninety-five per cent of planet on fire – dry, no water or rich vegetation to support Viriddion or animal life on surface - only a few small animals living underground in small damp hollows.

Viridis 6000 Status: ... The size of a football pitch and three floors deep; it accommodated one hundred and twenty passengers, made up of adults and children from thirty families; fully self-sufficient: producing food and clothing. All passengers were trained to pilot and maintain the ship, its produce and its equipment.

Flight Status:

One Month ... ... Family units preparing plans for Earth settlement .... Communication and Inter-actionist family unit preparing plans for special Earth Expedition to obtain specific animal data and search for missing E-Contacts....

Sixth Month ...... Flight going well ...... Children attending animal studies with their parents ...... Old Ridoros spending more time in the field than studying animals with parents and children .... Crew comfortable with controls....

Eighth Month ...... Many of the family and crew suffering with sickness ...... Sickness unidentified cause, query unidentified virus ...... Forty deaths, mostly adults leaving many children parent-less...

Tenth Month ...... No sign of sickness ...... Old Ridoros, still alive, refuses to move from the field   Some of the vacant crew positions have been taken over by the older children ......Special Expedition taken over by four young children mentored by two older children Klitheosia and Yanusanthio ...... Earth landing planned in one month ...... No decision for further Earth settlement until Special Expedition completed....

Eleventh Month ...... Arrived on Planet Earth in darkness ...... Ship trialled atmospheric cloaking to deter detection ..... Viridis 6000 placed under ice shelve ....

When Captain Genesis removed his Visionars, the pain and suffering over the past eleven months of the sick and now surviving children, was greater than he had ever experienced in his life before.

He was only in his early thirties but felt that his age had trebled. He was surely now ready to sleep...

He suddenly became aware of Klitheosia looking at him. She had in fact been watching him for a while. She had noticed how good looking he was even when he was so unshaven and unclean. Not wanting to disturb him and being about to leave, she noticed that he had caught sight of her.

"Captain Genesis, sorry to wake you but the children are planning to hold the departure meeting. Do you want to be involved?"

"Klitheosia, can you just give me another hour. I won't be any good to them like this!"

Klitheosia reassuringly backed away. She wanted to remind him that her registered Earth name was Elizabeth, just like his name was Robert Genesis, although she wouldn't mind hers being shortened to Beth, but as she left, she pressed the red button outside his room which would remind the crew to only disturb him in an emergency.

Beth was in fact Captain Genesis younger sister. She was not the youngest as he had another sister two years younger than Beth called Julie.

However, Beth, unlike him, had suddenly found herself in a hierarchy role by playing parent to the younger children chosen for the special expedition outside their spaceship and being in charge of their departure plans.

Captain Genesis, Beth and Julie's parents had both died with the sickness but their Grandfather, whom they called Old Ridoros, was still very much alive, although acting a little strange of late.

As she entered the communal room, she looked around the children that Luke, alias Yanusanthio, and her had chosen to accompany them on the Earth expeditions. She noticed, with some relief, that little Lithanisha had stopped crying.

Lithanisha was only six years old and the youngest child to be chosen. She had wept and sobbed for days alongside her dying Mother and then her Father. For weeks after, Beth had needed to gather her up in her arms and lay her into her lounger with her Visionars on the memory and comfort zone.

Whilst Beth reflected upon those days, she remembered how choosing little Lithanisha had therefore been a very difficult decision. Not for lack of animal communication skills, for she was the daughter of a chosen Viriddion line of proven animal inter-actionists.

No, Lithanisha's skills would never be in doubt, although, Lithanisha herself would need to work to develop that genetic knowledge and learn about the appropriate time to use it, but her health could be in doubt.

Viriddion's internal organs are on the right hand side of their bodies in contrast to Earthlings bodies whose mainly lie on the left and, although this in itself did not raise a problem, Lithanisha's organs needed to mature and would normally be slowly exposed to different atmospheric gases and pressures. So the journeys over land or while the sun was high, would need to be kept short.

"Children I know we're all getting excited about the work we have to do but it is important that the Captain is part of our planning. Whilst we wait I suggest we get on with the departure checks. Luke has a wrist Vigil for each of us".

Luke took the six Vigils, which all had different coloured straps. He placed them on their wrists ensuring he placed the yellow strapped one on Lithanisha, following her insistence that yellow was her favourite colour and that it should go on no one else.

Luke then went on to remind them that the Vigils "... were designed to be used as very simple communication devices between each other with one or two laser games incorporated ...... they looked very similar to Earth's automatic watches, which self-rewound on movement but, if they pressed particular buttons on the face of the watch, it would alert another member of the group for help ... ...the time had been synchronised with Earth Greenwich Mean Time which also showed the date and year".

Luke again reminded them that, once they had left, they would have no contact with Viridis 6000, although the ship would be able to monitor their positions and health conditions from their wrist Vigils because, constant signals from their position on Earth to the Viridis 6000 could alert the Earth authorities to their position under the ice.

"Now", ordered Beth, "Luke will start logging your discharge. When he calls out your Viriddion names, you must call back the name that your family has registered you as on Earth by the Earth Contact (E-Contact), which you will be known by from now on. As already explained the earthlings will find our Viriddion names very odd and the less that brings attention to ourselves, the better".

Luke reached for the audio pen to commence the name logging. "Listaylak".

Listaylak poised for thought. She was fourteen years old, with beautiful flowing typical Viriddion red hair. Of course, it wasn't flowing today. Beth had said that her hair must be tied back. She was also concerned about the clothing they had to wear.

Listaylak considered them very un-smart. Of course,

she understood the reason for having their uniforms made on Viridis 6000 from recycled waste vegetation grown in the ship field. Viridis council had made a decision centuries ago for each ship to be self-sufficient, as natural power and rich vegetation fields on the surface of Viridis began to decrease.

"Listaylak, your name please", Luke prompted.

"Tayla Windsor. No, it's not a boy's name, before you make comment", Tayla exclaimed directing a glare at the boys, as if she could read their thoughts. "My Mother wanted to name me after my Earth Great Great Grandfather. He was a Taylor who worked with very fine fabrics with very posh people".

"Who us! Never", grinned the boys is unison.

"Lithanisha, name please?"

Lithanisha shuffled off her stall. She had seen one of the maintenance crew return from his inspection of the outside of the ship. He had brought in a container which was full of some cold white hard stuff. Running her hands through the content she shouted with glee "Snow".

"No" responded Nathan. "This is ice. It probably was snow. Snow is much softer and younger".

"Come on children, you need to concentrate", continued Luke. "Jiorthansha, name please".

"Jimmy Penn".

"Mirothanshio, name please".

"George, Penn".

The little six year old rushed back to her stall between the twin brothers being inquisitive as always.

"Where did you get those names from?"

"Jimmy Carter and George Washington were famous

heads of state in America. Our Father was from Washington in America. He always said that we would love America and he was looking forward to showing us and mother around".

The twins suddenly became very sad looking, as they remembered their parents were no longer alive but, then realising that Snow had detected their sadness they quickly tried to change the subject "Why did your mother call you Snow?"

"She said, when I was born my hair was as white as Snow! But I've never seen snow".

"Don't worry about that", said George "You'll see lots and lots of it soon".

"S n o w S e y m o u r" ..., she slowly whispered her name back to herself. Then she quickly covered her face with her hands as she shyly and cautiously looked around to see if anyone else would question the reason behind her name; after all, it wasn't after a famous figure head that she could recollect.

After the discharge logging was completed and whilst they waited for Captain Genesis to see them off, the children amused themselves by testing out their wrist Vigils.

Snow was concerned that the laser might hurt her if she got in the way of it and the twins enlightened her to the Viriddion's laser game technology being invisible to the eye and harmless to human contact. Jimmy and George pressed buttons on their wrist Vigils and demonstrated a one to one, no contact tag around Snow.

"The game would be even better if we could have a Vigil

on both wrists" smiled Jimmy "But they're only allowing us one on this trip". "Yes, shame" agreed George.

Snow smiled to herself as she watched the boys play tag around her. To her, they were identical twins but they were adamant and insisted that they were not. It was true Jimmy always wore his hair parting on the opposite side to George's but Snow felt certain that they changed their parting sides over to occasionally confuse her.

Jimmy and George argued that they were mirror twins, saying that Jimmy had everything on his left and George had everything on this right.

Whatever that really meant, she wasn't sure, although she couldn't deny the fact that they both had a distinct little fleck of red hair on opposites sides of their foreheads amongst their thick mop of brown hair.

Meanwhile, Captain Genesis had stirred and focused on the five messages on the screen above his lounger:

1. Beth, Luke, Tayla, Jimmy, George and Snow ready to go.
2. Logan brothers waiting discharge orders.
3. Doc Thomas in Medical requests urgent counsel.
4. Roger from Intelligence requests urgent counsel.
5. Maintenance and Engineering Units requesting counsel.

As he began to read the messages he smiled and mused at the thought of the children logging their Earth names for discharge but, as he began to go through the list, his amusement changed to concern as he noted so many families requesting counsel.

His concern then changed to despair as he noticed the Intelligence request, as that could only imply one thing at this time: that they had not managed to land without being detected. Of course, his chances of landing on Earth, undetected, were practically zero but he had hoped otherwise.

Why Maintenance and Engineering Units were requesting counsel, he had no idea.

Suddenly, Captain Genesis's despair turned to panic, as he realised the urgency to get the children off the ship.

As he entered the departure lounge, he couldn't help smile again as he encountered the excitement of the children but, in contrast, couldn't help noticing Beth and Luke's expression of apprehension.

"Now children, you know your mission is to carry out the observation of various animals, look for a missing E-Contact and report back here as to whether you feel the families on Viridis 6000 could settle on Earth .....

Remember, your families have taught you well and their wisdom and spirit will be very much with you .....

Pilot Liam Logan and Co-Pilot Brandon Logan will take you in the multi-transporter to your first E-Contact. Each one of you have different observations and recordings to carry out. Jimmy and George, the Tiger. Tayla, the Zebra and Snow, the Polar Bear.....

Remember, you will need to acclimatise to the oxygen concentration level in the atmosphere, although the ships atmospherics have been slowly adjusting to mirror the Earth's atmosphere, since leaving Planet Viridis.....

Also remember, you can't take your Visionars but your right temple pulse will provide a little extra family reflection and comfort at times of stress and, although you cannot contact the ship, we will be able to keep an eye on you. May your families' blessings go with you".

And: with a sense of pride and as a sign of clearance for the children to go he clinched his left hand and then raised it in the Viriddion "V" across his chest.

He watched Jimmy and George, with Snow in tow, run off through the door of the multi-transporter, which was transformed at present into a mini-submarine to begin the journey. He couldn't help wondering whether they had made a mistake by allowing Snow to go so soon, considering her immature lung and heart development.

Beth must have read his thoughts, as she touched him on the shoulder saying "Don't worry, dear brother where's the Viriddion in you!"

As the crew closed the sub door the children settled in their seats. The transporter was very small. It only had eight seats, set in pairs, with a narrow walkway through the middle and Jimmy and George made a bee-line for the two seats behind Liam and Brandon's front seats.

Once released from Viridis 6000 the transporter stayed submerged as it proceeded through the North Atlantic waters towards a small harbour in the West of Scotland.

Large portals surrounding the sub provided live entertainment from the Arctic Ocean life as they inquisitively peered through to the children.

Tayla and Snow had insisted on sitting on the pair of seats behind the boys and so Beth and Luke were left to sit in the back two seats.

"Snow is there a problem?" requested Beth, as she could see Snow fidgeting in her seat in front of her.

"No, it's all right Beth; I'm just sorting my bag out".

"What are you doing in there Lemmie", she whispered, "I told you to stay in my lounger until I got back. Now you'll have to stay put. Don't show your face or Beth will be angry and make us go back".

Meanwhile, Tayla was busy looking at her new image in the reflection of the ocean portal, on her side, while Jimmy and George were begging Liam and Brandon to explain the odd sounds coming from the sub controls.

"That sound is letting us know that there is a ship above us and it's not far away. It doesn't appear to have picked us up on its radar yet, so we need to keep out of its range. We were informed about Russian and American Ships present in the Arctic, so it's going to be a hide and seek situation for a while".

Tayla continued to be absolutely fixated on her clothes. She was running her fingers over the denim trousers and found herself thinking deeply about her parents and how her Father had been in charge of the materials grown and manufactured on the University Control Ship and then on the Viridis 6000.

Both her Earth Father and Viriddion Mother had died from the recent virus. Tayla had been told by others that she was very much like her Viriddion Grandmother and, as she began to think upon her Mother, she could feel her combing her hair and saying "You've got your Grandmother's beautiful hair".

Suddenly Tayla's day dream was broken by the sound of Brandon shouting "Contact...Contact" and Liam, as he stopped the engine, simultaneously, demanded "Children, call the sea life to the sub".

Without hesitation, the children, Beth and Luke placed

their hands on the ocean portals and within seconds thousands of sea life surrounded the sub. Liam allowed the sub to be swept along by the sea life for a few minutes and then, when they were outside the ships radar, he re-started the sub and slowly moved it under the nearby ice ridge.

"Contact broken, well done children. Hopefully the crew on Viridis 6000 picked up on our engine being shut off, as a warning signal about a ship close by. And, hopefully we've been seen, by the ship above as a large shawl of fish".

The sub continued on its journey. The Viriddion children had only seen so much water on their Visionars and there was general excitement when a seal kept looking through the portal at Jimmy. However, it wasn't long before the children rested back exhausted.

Beth's responsible and concerned eyes looked over the children and noted that Snow had found some sort of comfort by placing her hand deep into her bag, which she was clutching tightly on her lap.

As Beth rested back, she caught a glimpse of Luke's piecing blue eyes gazing at her. She thought if she turned and looked at him, he might see how that last event had frightened her and the last thing she wanted to do was to give him the impression that she wasn't strong enough for the mission. So she closed her eyes and pretended she was resting them.

Luke, not only wanted Beth to look at him, to reassure her that he was there for her but he wanted to put his hand out and take hers. He and Beth had grown up together and he knew how she put on a brave exterior in times of trouble but, he had great respect for her and he remembered his feelings of honour and excitement when the Ships Council had elected him to accompany Beth and the children. So as he too rested back, he continued to listen to the radar sounds coming from the front.

"We are now approaching Oban harbour. The water depth will become too shallow for a sub to stay submerged and it will be easily identified as an "unidentified object" if the sub emerges to the surface. So, as the sub emerges we will slowly transform the outside to look more like a regular motor boat but as we reach a slipway I will put the wheels down and we will look like a large people or family carrier as we leave the water. We will then proceed on land to the Glenccuitten House, where they will be expecting us. It is dark and one o'clock in the morning, so hopefully the town will be sleepy and not too interested in us"

The children listened intensely to Liam and then looked at each other in fear as they again began to realise the cat and mouse aspect of their journey but, said nothing.

They gazed at the harbour lights as they approached and at the fishing boats bobbing up and down in their anchored positions alongside them. They had only seen such forms of water transport via their Visionars, for Viridis's water had long been dried up from the planet surface.

"Oo, er, look to the right everyone but don't make a sound children" whispered Brandon.

As the motor boat began to transform into a people carrier, it had ran up the slipway just a few feet away from a couple of men sitting on an old bench. They seemed to have some bottles in their hands and were talking loudly. One of them noticed the boat turn into a people carrier and shouted to the other to look. The other man was a little slow off the mark and, as he turned, he stood and tripped over his own feet and landed on his face in the opposite direction. The first man then found what the other man had done hysterically funny and on trying to help his mate up, ended up sprawled on top of him.

The children also found this hysterically funny. Even Liam and Brandon looked at each other, in utter amazement and tried to keep their laughter silent. Beth, well she was just pleased to see the children happy and Luke found himself relaxing just a little, as he saw a slight smirk on Beth's face.

The black people carrier continued to wind through the hills and narrow, snow banked, quiet roads towards Glenccuitten. They didn't pass many vehicles but when they did, they hadn't looked that odd or different.

It wasn't long before they reached a set of large high gates that appeared to magically open as the carrier approached and Liam drove straight up the drive and into a large garage as doors automatically closed behind them.

"Welcome to Glenccuitten, my name is Rubin McDonald and I trust you had a good journey".

The passengers tumbled out of the carrier and introduced themselves one by one, to a very smartly dressed gentleman, with a very cheerful smile.

"You must be very tired; I'll take you to your rooms and send Martha up with some food and drink. Then you must get some sleep. I have to go into the government office in the morning but we can talk when I return".

They followed the gentleman up some large winding

stairs to three beautifully prepared rooms. All of the visitors looked absolutely amazed at each other and there was only one thought that went through their minds "So this is what a house is really like".

Again, a house was only something seen via their Visionars because all of them had been born and brought up on a spaceship, the Viridis 6000.

It wasn't long before Martha brought up some food and drink which they downed very quickly. She was a quietly spoken lady about the same age as Rubin, with thick rich red hair drawn back in a bun and she reassured them that she would see them in the day room down stairs in the morning.

"Snow, why are you putting the apple in your bag? Do you not want it?"

"Yes, it's all right Beth. I'm a bit full at the moment. I'll have it in the morning!"

They all settled down in their rooms. Liam and Brandon in one room, Beth, Tayla and Snow in another with Luke and the twins in the third.

When Beth switched the lights off she noticed that Snow had taken her bag to bed with her but she thought that if it could give her some comfort, she'd leave it with her. But, it wasn't long before she heard the sound of an apple being crunched.

"Snow!"

"Sorry Beth. I've changed my mind. I'm still hungry. I won't be long", she said pulling the covers up over her, trying to cut the noise down from Lemmie eating her apple.

TWO

CAPTAIN GENESIS

Since the children had left the ship, Captain Genesis had held counsel with all of the families, which included the Medical and Intelligence Units. The situation was clearly very grave. The heads of families were now young and obviously very fearful for the future of their sibling relations and for themselves.

The Medical Unit had not been able to identify the virus that had caused the death of the older Viriddions' and the Intelligence Unit had clear evidence that the ship had been seen entering Earth's atmosphere. In addition, the Maintenance and Engineering Units believed they needed to join forces to keep the ship safe, due to the reduced crew.

The question that kept coming to Captain Genesis was "What shall I do. If I take the ship back up and leave Earth,

I will be abandoning the children to fend for themselves. And, if they should be caught by any one of the Earth's Governments or Armies, they might be imprisoned even tortured".

After all the Earth's perception of visitors from other planets was generally around: little green men with intent to take over the Earth!

At that point, he had to stop thinking on those lines. But, what are the alternatives? Some families had suggested that they leave the ship. They argued that, if the ship couldn't leave its place under the ice, then they had no alternative but to make their home on Earth.

However, as Captain Genesis had pointed out, that since the recent deaths the only pilots able to take a transporter out were the Logan brothers and they were with the children.

The Viridis 6000 had five other transporters but the student pilots still needed supervising, which could only be done if the Logan brothers returned.

No, he had only one way to go. He had to get his Grandfather, Old Ridoros, out of the field. He needed him alongside when he held the next counsel. If anyone could reassure the young families that things will work out, it would be Ridoros.

Ridoros sat quietly and listened as his Grandson paced up and down, pouring out his heart. He looked at his strong outline which reminded him of himself when he was in George V's Cavalry but he also saw a passion to save life, which he loved in his Viriddion wife.

How could he reassure the young families that the children would be safe? How could he reassure them that all will be well? He, of all people, knew the thinking of the Earth people because he once thought like them.

"Grandfather, if you can't do it for me, please do it for Beth".

"Beth"

"Klitheosia, my younger Sister. Your Granddaughter. She's out there with the children. She needs to know we're here for her".

Ridoros could take the pleading no more. "All right, I'll come in from the field but I can't wave a magic wand".

Sure enough, at the next counsel, Ridoros stood strong and protective. He reassured the families that the mission had not changed. That the dangers had not changed from what they were when they elected to leave Viridis; only that a lot of them had lost their parents. The wisdom and experience of their parents would still be stored in the Viridis's University Control Ship, which they could obtain through their Visionars at any time: and that they must use them when needed.

He continued to outline their main mission of supporting the children whilst they searched for the missing E-Contacts and as they monitored the health of certain animals.

Ridoros reminded them that, up until five years ago, Viridis had six E-Contacts living on Earth who kept in contact with Viridis. They ensured that the children born on Viridis who had Earth parents or grandparents, were registered on Earth in case they needed to make their home on Earth when Planet Viridis couldn't sustain life any longer.

E-Contacts were men or women originally from Earth who had spent time studying on Planet Viridis and who had returned to Earth to share their knowledge within their employed positions and to continue to provide safe houses for Viriddion visitors.

Ridoros continued to remind them that: this situation had continued on for thousands of years and because most of the Viriddions' have Earth genealogy now, they presumably are all Earth registered. However, the loss of contact with two E-Contacts may have put the collection of some of the Earth birth certificates, in jeopardy, making it impossible for some children to make their home legally on Earth.

Ridoros began to sway about and he felt faint. He had to get back to the field. He didn't really know why but, of late, he felt he could breathe better there. But, he wasn't going to let his Grandson down. So he continued "...Trust Captain Genesis, if any person can get you settled on Earth safely he can" and as he slumped to his chair he muttered "I and his Grandmother have trained him and his parents well"

"Grandfather!"

"Genesis, don't take me to Medical, take me back to the field".

Captain Genesis knew better than to disobey his Grandfather and immediately complied with his wishes.

The field was not very large even though it was the largest compartment in the ship. It grew certain vegetables and fruit and farmed a few sheep and goats. He had spent many hours talking to his Grandfather there.

When Captain Genesis was much younger, he remembered asking his Grandfather about the planet Earth and whether it would have a field on it like this on Viridis 6000. After chuckling for some time, his reply had been that the field on Viridis 6000 was very tiny compared to Earth fields and, in fact, it was no larger than a football pitch.

Captain Genesis, at that time, had not seen the funny side but as he had grown older and learnt more about the Earth and about various games played on Earth, he began to appreciate the reason for his Grandfather's chuckle.

So he wasn't that surprised that his Grandfather felt at home there but still, a great relief come over him, when a member of the crew returned to say that Ridoros had taken a drink of tea and said he was feeling much better.

Captain Genesis made a call to Roger in Intelligence. "I need to know exactly what you know".

Roger Baker was in his early forties. He had been elected Head of Intelligence, after his Father had died five year ago. It was a natural line of promotion, as he had worked alongside and been trained in Intelligence by his Father, ever since he could walk and talk, just as his Father, Douglas Baker originally from America, before him.

Similarly, Roger had his daughter Sarah working alongside him, who had been able to take over control, when he had contracted the strange virus that had caused the death of so many of the older crew but, which he had recovered from.

"Captain, I can tell you exactly what the Americans and Russians are thinking because our equipment is so more advanced than theirs. I can even let you hear them discuss their sightings about us and plans for us but, what we cannot avoid, is that, whilst we sit here under the ice, we are sitting ducks waiting to be slaughtered. It would only take one depth charge to hit us from a ship above and we are finished. The hit may only dent our ship but it would disrupt the atmospherics and .... then ....."

"Ok ok, I get the picture. Where's the real threat at the moment?"

Roger gave the Captain a red set of headphones and offered him a seat. "You listen to this and make your own mind up, whilst I just check a few other things out".

As the Captain rested back, he could hear three voices, all men. One man was concerned about an Unidentified Flying Object (UFO) report. Not because the report was about a UFO as their office received sightings from the public on a regular basis, but because the sighting was reported by one of their officers, who was in fact on her honeymoon in Scotland.

Another man had joked about whether it was an expected effect of a honeymoon to see flying saucers in the night sky. The third man laughed and suggested that, in the circumstances, they should just sit on it to see if further reports are made. But, the first man to speak suggested that they should make some enquiries from their agents in the north to demonstrate to Officer Twine that her report had been taken seriously.

Roger made a little adjustment on his monitor and the Captain heard another set of Intelligence. It appeared that an Unidentified Underwater Object (UUO) had been reported by one of the Russian ships on one of its routine patrols in the Arctic. Apart from a suggestion of a sea monster or stray whale they agreed that it was more likely to be an American spy sub. So the outcome was to increase their patrols and be alert to any strange and odd movement in the area.

Captain Genesis took the headphones off. "Well, it appears, we may have a little thinking time. Let me know as soon as the situation changes".

"Captain, did you recognise one of the American voices?"

"Yes. Does the voice trace identify him as our American E-Contact?"

"Positive".

"Good, we may need him; meanwhile I need to speak to the Medical Unit".

Captain Genesis made his way to the Medical Unit, where Doc Thomas reassured him that Ridoros was definitely feeling a lot better since returning to the field.

"Doc Thomas, are we any the wiser about the virus, that caused the deaths of our parents?"

"No: but we won't give up. We're still awaiting the outcome of some tests. I'll let you know as soon as we know something further. Meanwhile, I'll keep an eye on your Grandfather.

Actually, we don't think it was a virus", smiled Doc Thomas. "The thing is we haven't really had this situation before. Normally if we visit earth, we are transferring or collecting one or two people and therefore we have only adjusted the atmospherics of a few rooms. And, in addition, the persons being transferred or collected are normally between twenty and forty years old, unless they are an Earth person."

"So, what are you trying to tell me?"

"It is possible that Ridoros escaped death because he followed his instincts. He found he could breathe better in the field, suggesting that the gasses from the greenery, trees, bushes and animal fodder offset the atmospheric changes in the field and therefore did not affect Ridoros lungs as much as the other older crew members. This could be demonstrating that older people's lungs can't adapt to the atmospheric changes as easily as a younger pair of lungs. But: I am only guessing at the moment."

Horrified by the reasoning, the Captain exploded, "Are you saying, we killed our parents?"

"There was nothing in the medical writings against the introduction of Earth's atmospheric pressures on the more mature lung. We had made adjustments before with no ill effects, albeit with young people. No such illness has been reported by the other ships which have settled on other planets

We only knew that young lungs take a little while to develop and to be able to make minor atmospheric adjustments. But, we had no knowledge that once the lungs reach a certain maturity they would be unable to make those adjustments. This situation was inevitable, after making the decision to make our life on earth. In any event, it could still be a virus we have not come across before!"

"Maybe, but, at the moment, we don't know whether we are here to stay!"

Captain Genesis returned to the bridge. He couldn't believe the situation they were in. He was happier that the young family units had settled down a little and he kept telling himself that he should be relaxing more but, something kept niggling him about the Intelligence Officer Twine. "Who was she? How dangerous could she be? And: where exactly was she now?"

He had asked Roger Baker to find out more about her but the only information they had gathered was that she had recently joined the UFO Office and was a very intelligent and dedicated officer in her late thirties.

She had lost her parents in a car crash when she was five, brought up in an orphanage and recently married to a Winston Stirwell, a freelance reporter from Houston who was also brought up in the same orphanage with Gwendoline Twine.

"Captain, we've been monitoring the children's heart beats. They are all sleeping well at the moment but Snow appears to have another heart beat alongside hers. It's too fast for a human!"

"Does it appear to be unsettling her?"

"No, in fact just the opposite"

"I expect the place where they are staying has one of those house cats and it has made itself comfortable on Snow. Just keep an eye on it; they'll be waking up soon".

THREE

SNOW'S E-FRIEND

Snow felt the presence of Lemmie under her chin and for a moment thought she was back on the ship in her lounger.

She thought she could sense: the yellow and orange light reflections on her walls and lockers, from the horizontal tubular light to the corner of her lounger; the odd voice of a crew member in the distance; and her Mother and Father discussing their plans for the day in their room adjoined to hers.

Then she saw daylight coming through between the curtains of the room and remembered … "Lemmie", she whispered, "you must get back in the bag".

"Snow, come on, I thought you'd never wake up. The others have gone down for breakfast".

When Beth took Snow's hand and led her down stairs

and through into the morning room, she was somewhat taken back by the sight of other people sitting at various tables having their breakfast and she found herself bowing her head in shyness as she passed them by.

She made her way to a large table, set for eight, where Luke and the other children sat. The table was placed in the corner of the room next to a bay window that overlooked a large garden. It was rich with bushes, trees, shrubs and thick green grass that was slowly being covered by white flakes falling from the sky.

This again was a sight which the visitors from Viridis had only seen in pictures and described in archaic writing thousands of years old.

The lady called Martha, who brought them supper to their rooms the night before, gave Beth a large brown envelope and explained that the two drivers, Liam and Brandon had their breakfast earlier and were in the garage servicing the people carrier.

Beth placed the envelope on the table beside her. She really wanted to open it immediately but, she felt the priority was to get the children to order their breakfast. However, what would normally be a simple task for her was proving very difficult, as they appeared absolutely transfixed on the falling snow.

With the strange people around her Beth didn't want to bring attention to herself and the children, so she quietly apologised to Martha. Martha appeared to understand the dilemma Beth was in and gently took over the situation.

"Come, come children, tell me what you want for breakfast and I'm sure your parents will let you go and play in the garden with Penny, when you've finished".

"Can we, p l e a s e", they all voiced together with excitement, looking backwards and forwards between Beth and Luke.

"Yes, if you do as Martha suggests and eat your breakfast".

Needless to say, breakfast was ordered and every scrap was eaten very quickly and the children were soon in the garden with Penny.

Penny was a friendly eight year old with long mousy coloured plaits, neatly tied at the ends with red ribbons. She told the children that she was Rubin McDonald's granddaughter and that she lived with her grandfather in this hotel and, as she had a day off from school, she was going to make a snowman and then play with her doll.

So it wasn't long before they were all running and rolling about in the soft white snow as it fell around them. Penny showed the boys how to roll the snow into large balls and lift them carefully on top of each other.

As Penny looked around for large stones and sticks that could make the snowman's eyes, nose and mouth, a couple of doves settled on a garden seat to see what was going on and, before long, a young deer had hopped the fence into the garden and nudged Tayla in her back, making her jump. Taylor immediately responded by dabbing some snow on his nose and then whispered something in his ear.

Jimmy and George had lifted up a couple of rabbits that had popped out the shrubbery and Snow was engrossed with a little robin that kept sitting on her shoulder.

Beth and Luke, who had been sitting in silence proudly watching the children play and interact with the local animals, suddenly became aware of raised voices in the morning room from other visitors having their breakfast.

"Gosh, aren't the animals in Scotland really friendly?"

"The animals must be extra hungry and the children must have taken food out in their pockets!"

"Oh, Winston, I would love to stroke a deer, can we take some food out?"

"The snow is really falling quite heavy love, you might get a chill. In any event, Gwendoline we've got a train to catch and then the plane back to America".

"Ok dear; I suppose you're right" sighed Gwendoline.

Meanwhile, Beth had called the children back in, and after drying themselves down, they excitedly returned to their table with Beth and Luke.

Snow trailed behind and as she passed by Gwendoline she smiled and Gwendoline said "Hello, I love your bag. Did you have food in there for the Robin?"

"No, just my friend" and began to open her bag to show the lady.

Gwendoline had a constantly enquiring mind and became very inquisitive at this point. Finding Snow very friendly she wanted to talk to her more, especially after hearing Martha refer to the two older ones of the group as the children's parents and then noting that the eldest child, out of the four children looked about sixteen, she couldn't stop herself from asking Snow whether they were her parents.

"No, that's Beth and Luke our teachers. They teach us about animals"

"Oh, don't your parents mind you going on holiday with your teachers?"

"No, all our parents have died" said Snow sadly and, at that point, decided not to show the lady her friend in her bag and continued to make her way to the table.

"Oh Winston, did you hear that. They're on holiday from an orphanage".

"Sounds much nicer than ours was dear! Our holidays were having occasional tea and cakes with the Vicar's wife, in their house next door. Do you remember?"

"Sure. I wonder what orphanage they're from!"

The morning room slowly cleared and Beth opened the envelope which she had been given. Inside were eight birth certificates, which included one for Liam and Brandon, eight corresponding passports, bank card with her name on and a letter which read:

> *"Dear Beth. I am unable to see you as planned. You must leave Glenccuitten immediately for Kittila in Finland. Your escorts Liam and Brandon have the contact address and will choose the best route to get you there. The card, which you know all about, will allow you to draw cash from Banks or their Automatic Teller Machines, as you need it. Trust we will meet again – R.M."*

Beth felt a strange feeling come over her as she looked at the births certificates. Her feelings were mixed with a sense of relief and shame. She, of course, realised the importance for every person on Earth to have a birth certificate and passport if they needed to travel to different places on Earth and, therefore, felt a relief that, at least, all of them on this visit now had theirs.

However, when she had sight of Liam and Brandon Logan's birth certificates, she began to realise how she hadn't given the brothers much thought, since leaving the ship, possibly because the Logan brothers were from the Sub-Marina/Aero-physics and Aviation Academy in Viridis.

Liam was only twenty and Brandon Logan was only eighteen but because they had also lost their parents on the Viridis 6000, they had no option but to take on their Father's pilot role. They too, like Roger Baker in Intelligence, had trained alongside their Father for as long as they could remember.

Beth reflected on the Logan brothers and reminded herself of her responsibility to take care of not only of the younger ones but the older ones in their group visiting Earth.

She gave Luke the envelope and content to read, whilst she ushered the children to collect their things from their rooms to make themselves ready to leave.

Back in her bedroom, as Snow was making sure Lemmie was comfortable in her bag, she noticed Penny at her door.

"Snow, where do you live?"

"On another planet called Viridis".

"Are you going back now?"

"No, I don't think so"

"Do you want to see my doll, before you go?" asked Penny holding out a china doll, colourfully dressed about 20 centimetres tall.

Snow took the doll in her hand and ran her fingers gently over and down her long blonde hair. She had only seen pictures in her Visionars of such pretty dolls. Viridis had not manufactured such items for thousands of years, due to the need to manufacture essential items of living only. "She has beautiful long hair, just like Mother's, except my Mother's hair was flame-red like that" pointing to Tayla's hair.

Penny noticed the sadness in Snow's voice and wanted to say something to cheer her up. "My Grandfather said your Mother had died recently. You can live here with me if you like and share my Mother!"

Snow smiled, she didn't really know Penny but already she felt comfortable and safe with her. She flung her arms around Penny and wanted to say yes but she said "You can be my best E-Friend".

Penny appeared happy with that. She wasn't certain exactly what that meant but intended to ask her Grandfather later. She wasn't concerned that her new friend was from another planet because her Grandfather had often told her that there could be other Earth's with people living on them.

Within an hour they were all on their way to Kittila, a Lapland village in Finland in a helicopter: a helicopter which Liam and Brandon had now transformed the transporter into.

The helicopter flew over the hills, around snow topped mountains and the children pointed out strange large ships as they crossed the North Sea from Scotland towards Finland.

To Beth and Luke's relief the children were cheerful

and they were able to relax a little now they weren't with other strangers. The children happily chatted about the animals they had en-counted in the Hotel garden, Martha the housemaid and the smart cheerful gentleman called Rubin McDonald and his granddaughter Penny.

Liam and Brandon told them that Rubin had informed them he was in regular contact with their Scottish Grandfather, James Logan. Apparently, their Grandfather had returned to Scotland as an E-Contact, after their Viriddion Grandmother had died.

He was in his nineties and, over the past couple of years, had become very frail and forgetful. However, it hadn't helped when asked by various health visitors about whether he had any family, he had told them that they lived on another planet but would be visiting him soon. So they placed him in a Care Home for the elderly in Grangemouth.

Rubin had explained that, although he was born on Viridis, he had an Earth Grandfather and therefore chose to come to Earth with old James Logan to work alongside him as an E-Contact.

He also reassured the Logan brothers that their Grandfather was safe and that perhaps they could visit him when they returned.

Martha had packed the visitors a lunch which included a small pack of chocolate buttons for the four children.

"Wow, we've read about chocolate, haven't we? I'm going to hold on to my packet for as long as possible, until I can't resist them any more", laughed Jimmy promptly opening them.

So the journey continued until they finally landed in

a small back road about two miles from their destination. On landing, Liam and Brandon transformed the helicopter back to a people carrier and they continued their journey by road until they arrived at a little log cabin in Kittila at the end of the day.

They were all very tired and one by one fell instantly asleep the moment they had worked out who was going to sleep where, with Snow as usual taking her bag to bed with her.

FOUR

ALFIE AND ERNIE

Meanwhile, as the visitors from Viridis slept soundly, two men, on their evening off from dressing up as Santa's elf helpers, decided to break into the village Bank and filled a sack full of bank notes. Of course, it wasn't long before one of them triggered an alarm in the local Police Station. When they heard sirens and saw flashing lights, the off duty elves crept out of the back of the Bank via the hole in the wall, they had earlier made, and fled on a jet ski.

The elves fled back to Santa's grotto and continued to wrap up presents ready for the next day, as if nothing had happened. They thought they had successfully got away with the burglary but, to be on the safe side, they hid the sack of notes in one of the presents, so they could collect it later when things had calmed down.

The Police, on discovering the hole at the back of the

Bank followed the Jet Ski tracks from the village to Santa's grotto and began to methodically question Santa and the elves, one by one.

Inspector Moody, whose name clearly appeared to reflect his nature, was getting quite angry over the sudden pressure he and his men were under. Not only had he been informed about the bank robbery but he had been informed about a strange looking helicopter that had been seen flying towards his patch earlier that evening. He had to send some of his team out looking for a helicopter and any tyre tracks travelling to and or from a helicopter landing site, before too much snow fell.

FIVE

PLANNING A VISIT TO SANTA

Back in the log cabin, that morning, when the Viriddion visitors awoke, Beth informed them that they had a Zoo to visit but first they would visit Santa. She looked at Snow with a glint in her eye and smiled at the rest of the children.

"Do you mean, Father Christmas", said Snow.

"Yes, we thought, as Liam and Brandon have to carry out maintenance on the carrier, before continuing on, you might like to visit Santa and his elves".

"Oo, yes. Can I ask him for anything?"

"You could try", suggested Jimmy and George, grinning at each other.

Their discussion was interrupted by a knock at the door.

"Welcome, to Lapland. The snow is thick, so would you

like a sleigh ride into Santa's village", offered a round faced cheerful looking gentleman.

"Well", responded Beth "that's perfect timing. Have you got room for six of us?" and not waiting for a reply, Jimmy, George, Snow and Tayla were out and up into the sleigh before he could say no.

The sleigh was pulled by a couple of reindeer and Beth couldn't help stroking their noses and saying hello to them before stepping up into the back of the sleigh with the children, leaving Luke the honour of sitting in the front with the Lapland sleigh-man.

SIX

CAPTAIN GENESIS

Back on Viridis 6000 Captain Genesis had become increasingly concerned for Snow because the crew continued to inform him that she had an extra heart-beat, albeit with a beat much faster than her own would normally be.

His concern changed however and he didn't know whether to laugh or cry when one of the crew informed him that a young Slender Loris was missing from the veterinary unit. The crew member had said that Snow's Mother had been looking after it after putting its leg in plaster following a fracture and suggested that it was either loose in the ship and needed to be found or Snow had adopted it.

Captain Genesis rested his head in his hands in despair

"No, surely she hasn't. She wouldn't have. Yes, she has, hasn't she? I wonder whether Beth knows".

However, his despair was short lived when Roger from Intelligence called him to listen in on the American UFO department.

As before: Captain Genesis put on the headphones and heard a lady saying:

"Sir, I know, at least, the difference between a shooting star and an object flying through the atmosphere. No, I didn't see it land but, if I was in Scotland and it went over my head towards the North-West, it must have been seen by other people further up in the North Sea area".

"What exactly did it look like?" questioned the man she had been talking to.

"Admittedly it was dark. There were lots of clouds around because I didn't see many stars out. All I saw was what looked like a small cloud travelling in the opposite direction to the other clouds. I know our agent in the north has just reported a sighting of a UFO but that is at least two days later than when I saw it. It must be another one or they have got their days mixed up".

"Officer Stirwell-Twine," emphasizing her newly chosen double barrelled surname, "I think what you saw sounds more like a sighting of an unidentified cloud", laughed the man.

"Look, Sir, I know what I saw. There is something strange going on because Winston just called to tell me that a strange looking helicopter had been seen travelling towards Finland from the North Sea direction and that a bank in Finland had just had a break-in. He said he was on his way to Finland to cover the story and would keep me informed".

"Are you suggesting that we have been invaded by aliens who are using a helicopter to travel the Earth and break in our Banks? Changing the subject for the moment, did you have a nice honeymoon?"

"Yes thank you Sir. We stayed in a little village call Glenccuitten. It was quite a busy little hotel with a bunch of children and their teachers on holiday there from an orphanage. The youngest was about six and her name was Snow... .."

Captain Genesis put the headphones down. He thought he felt his heart miss a beat. He couldn't bear to listen any more. Clearly the American Intelligence lady was talking about the children. He desperately wanted to speak to Beth and the children to warn them about the helicopter sighting but he couldn't.

He felt isolated and useless but he was also concerned that Stirwell-Twine had also mentioned another UFO sighting two days after their landing. He wondered why he hadn't received a message from the American E-Contact but then remembered, whilst they were under the ice, the E-Contacts needed to stay silent.

All he and the crew could do for the children, at present, was check their well-being via their wrist Vigils and know where they were on the radar but, what good was that really to the children?

He just had to trust that the Logan brothers could keep a close eye on them.

There didn't seem to be any further activity or concern coming from the Russians or Americans above them in the

Arctic Ocean, so he thought he would spend a little time with his Grandfather in the field, bringing him up to date with the latest on Snow and her little companion.

SEVEN
_____

SANTA'S GROTTO

Back in Lapland, the children were busy looking around the village shops. Beth and Luke had decided that the children would probably have plenty of time to spend on the ski slopes in between the tasks they had to do and therefore had taken the children into a ski suit shop and had kitted them all out with appropriate warm suits and goggles.

The Viriddion visitors, being brought up on a spaceship, were used to being protected from extreme weather changes but Beth and Luke knew they needed to protect themselves from the coldness and brightness of the snow. They had spent time in a little shop having tea and cakes and were now off again in a sleigh to visit Santa and his elves.

Santa had a lot of visitors and Snow had to wait a little

while to see him. She was not at all unhappy about that because it gave her a little time to think about, what she was going to ask Santa for.

Beth and Tayla were slightly inquisitive about the grotto, so they said that they just wanted to keep Snow company, whilst Luke said he would stay and keep an eye on Jimmy and George who both wanted to stay outside and play snow missiles.

When Snow finally stepped forward to greet Santa, she couldn't help smiling and wanted to give him a big kiss. He was just like the Father Christmas pictures her Mother had shown her and she ran her hand over his bright red jacket and big black belt, as if she was making sure every item of clothing was in order according to the pictures. She looked down to his big black boots and thought "Yes, just like the picture. He must be very old!"

"Snow. What a lovely name. Come sit on my knee and tell me where you are from and what you would like more than anything for Christmas".

Snow whispered in his ear because she didn't want to upset Beth. "I'm from Planet Viridis and, can I have my Mother back, please?"

Santa looked hard into Snow's large, watery, piecing blue eyes, and felt sure he had looked upon them many years ago and the place she had mentioned sounded familiar but, his hearing and eye sight weren't as good as they used to be, so he surmised that he could have misheard her.

"Snow, there are some things that not even Santa can give you but, I have a present for you that I think might help you to remember your Mother" and he gave her a large box wrapped in colourful red shiny paper and sealed with a dark green ribbon tied in a bow.

Snow couldn't believe her eyes, she had never received such a large parcel before and after giving him another big kiss she ran off with the parcel to show Beth and Tayla.

Immediately outside, Snow told the boys all about Santa and began to open the parcel but Jimmy said "No, Snow, you mustn't open it before Christmas Day. You must look after it until then".

Snow looked a little disappointed but, as she looked around at George, Tayla, Beth and Luke they all seemed to agree, she settled for, at least, just being the owner of the special prettily wrapped parcel.

The children were just getting back into a sleigh, when a police car with flashing lights and sirens blaring pulled up outside the grotto and two officers stepped out and went into the grotto. People began to stop and watch, including the sleigh man and the next thing they saw was Santa being escorted into the police car and driven away.

"What was that all about?" Luke asked the sleigh man.

The sleigh man explained about the bank in the village being broken into the night before and said the newspapers, no doubt, will be full of it tomorrow morning and what Santa might have to do with it.

Once back at the chalet, after explaining their day to the Logan brothers, the Viriddion visitors settled down for the night. Snow placed her parcel at the end of her bed, so she could feel it with her feet every now and then and ensured Lemmie had his fruit.

EIGHT

ALFIE AND ERNIE

While the village and log cabin visitors slept, the off duty elves were busy looking through the presents in the grotto. They were looking for the present which held their sack of bank notes.

"Alfie was it this one?"

"No, it was much bigger than that. Ernie, look in that corner"

"What this one?"

"No, you nutcracker, that's much too big. I'm sure I placed it to the right of Santa, when he was speaking to that little blond one and I told him to take the present on his left. Do you think he gave her the present on the right?

"How do I know, you were the head elf, giving Santa the presents"

"Did you see which cabin in the village they are staying in?"

"No, but she may have told Santa".

"Oh yes, I'm sure Santa's going to want to talk to us now".

"The sleigh man might remember".

"Yes, of course Ernie, you're so clever".

NINE

VISIT TO POLICE STATION

Early the following morning, the Logan brothers ventured into the village and returned with a newspaper that had a large picture of Santa in handcuffs in the centre of two policemen. It read, "SANTA BURGLES BANK IN FRONT OF HIS ELVES". A freelance journalist called Winston Stirwell had reported that Santa had been seen breaking into the Bank by two of his elf workers and that the police were looking for possible accomplices whom he must have passed the bank notes on to and owners of a strange looking helicopter seen in the vicinity.

The children were shocked. Beth tried to explain to Liam and Brandon that Santa didn't look like a guy who would rob a bank but what could they do.

Liam and Brandon looked closely at the picture and noted that Santa was holding his left hand, raised across his chest with only his index finger and middle raised, similar to the Viriddion "help" sign. They showed this gesture to Beth and Luke and suggested that they take the children out skiing for the day, while they go to the police station to see if they could visit Santa.

"Ok, it's probably a coincidence but, we can't just walk away from the poor guy without checking him out. After all, Rubin sent us in this direction for a reason."

"Brandon, can you please give Santa his present back. I don't want him to get in trouble because of the present he gave me".

Brandon looked at Snow and then at the other children that were looking back at him, obviously wondering what he was going to say. "Look Snow, I'm sure it was nothing to do with the present he gave you but I'll look after it for you until we've at least spoken to Santa. That's if the police let us."

Snow and the others appeared happy with that and all of them wrapped themselves up well and walked very slowly through the snow to the village.

When they arrived, Beth and Luke took the children off to the ski slopes and Liam and Brandon made their way to the police station.

"Liam, how are we going to play this? You know we could end up behind bars with him?"

"Actually, I've no idea but, we've got to try".

"Yes", said an officer behind a desk.

"I'm Santa's brief and this is my clerk", said Liam nodding towards Brandon, very official like.

"I didn't know he had asked for one"

"Oh, come on, you know the rules, he doesn't need to.

Just tell him his lawyer is here. He either wants to see me or he doesn't".

The officer returned and showed them into a room where a tired looking old man with white hair and beard sat behind a desk.

As Liam and Brandon walked boldly up to the table with their left arms and hands raised across their chest in the Viriddion greeting position, they heard the officer lock the door behind them.

David Seymour sat transfixed at the sight of the young men. He had hoped that his Viriddion hand sign had been seen but he hadn't been expecting two young men. He wasn't aware of any E-Contacts who were so young therefore he wasn't certain whether he could trust them, even if they had greeted him with the Viriddion gesture. On the other hand, had he heard correctly from that little blond girl yesterday? Was it possible that Viridis 6000 had arrived!

He desperately wanted to return their greeting but he couldn't. He feared that an officer could be watching the interview from the other side of the mirrored window and the return greeting would become obvious and possibly put the lads in danger too.

"My name is Seymour. I'm innocent. I didn't break into any bank".

The brothers noted Seymour's eyes directing their attention to the mirrored window in the wall and knew their questions and answers had to be guarded.

"Have you any idea why the two elf workers have accused you of carrying out the robbery?"

Oh, David Seymour knew exactly why because that

was one of the reasons why he had been prevented from making his usual contact with Viridis.

He knew that he always tried to see the best in people and when two dubious characters asked to work as elves and assured him that they had changed their ways, he believed them. When they said they didn't have anywhere to live, he felt sorry for them and allowed them to stay in his cottage in the village until they got back on their feet.

When they next locked him out of his home, he felt he couldn't make a fuss about it, in case the police entered the cottage and discovered the E-Contact equipment. He wasn't that worried about the two elf workers, they weren't that bright and they would probably think that a box in the corner of his lounge marked [Sewing Machine] was just that.

"No, Alfred Pike and Ernest Pratt are my friends, or I thought they were, and they stay in my cottage in the village".

"Mr Seymour, we'll get the papers in place for your defence. The Insurance Company for the Bank are not likely to agree to a release while the money is still missing. We'll be in touch soon".

Liam and Brandon stood up to leave and, as an officer unlocked the door Liam reached over to shake Seymour's hand and he responded.

Liam gave the officer his mobile number before leaving and left strict instructions to be called, if the situation should change.

The brothers slowly walked back to the cabin. They had been given mobile phones by Rubin but, at that time, hadn't realised the importance or need for them. So they had put Rubin's number in them and now they added the police station number.

They continued to discuss what they should do next as it wasn't easy knowing what David Seymour wanted them to do. Although the newspaper had not named the witnesses who claimed they saw Santa breaking into the bank, David Seymour had clearly indicated that he thought it was the two living in his cottage named Alfred and Ernest.

When they opened the door to their log cabin, they couldn't believe their eyes. The place was in a terrible mess. Clothing was all over the floor, mattresses were turned upside down and carrier bags were emptied and contents sprawled everywhere.

"What the hec! Someone has been looking for something".

"Who, for what and did they find it? Liam, do you think we ought to report this to the police or keep this to ourselves for the moment. We don't want to worry the children. We could talk to Beth and Luke when the children are asleep".

"What about the transporter!"

The door from the cabin into the garage was locked firmly and outside the snow that had built up against the external doors had no fresh footprints. The brothers gave a big sigh of relief.

"What was so important that they didn't think of looking in the garage?" queried Brandon.

"I don't know but I think a telephone call to Rubin, would be a good start".

When the children returned, they returned to a very

tidy cabin and were full of their skiing trip. Jimmy and George said that a couple of Santa's elves had begun to teach them all how to ski and they were very impressed with Snow's sheer determination to stay upright.

Liam and Brandon showed a little concern when they heard the mention of Santa's elves but presumed that Santa had lots of working elves, all over the village.

"Alfie asked me whether I liked my present but, I told him I was keeping it until Christmas Day because I forgot I was giving it back. Did you give it back to Santa Brandon?"

Brandon knelt down alongside Snow, he wanted to tell her that he had met her Grandfather today but, because they couldn't be sure, he knew that this was not the right time. "No, it was not the right time to give it back. We'll think about it. Santa might be very sad if you give the present back and he is really a good Santa".

Beth and Luke settled the children down and, as hoped, Liam and Brandon told them about their meeting with David Seymour and the state of the log cabin when they returned.

TEN

CAPTAIN GENESIS

Meanwhile, back on Viridis 6000, the crew had called Captain Genesis to the bridge. They explained that whilst monitoring the group's vital signs, they had recorded a further heart-beat alongside Pilot Logan.

"Explain how that could be".

"We think he must have touched or shaken another person's hand, and the records show him as one of the missing E-Contacts, David Seymour".

"Oh, well done. They've found him. Is he well?"

"His vital signs are reasonable, although his heart beat is slightly elevated suggesting he is anxious about something".

Captain Genesis called up Intelligence on the large viewer on the bridge.

"Yes, Captain", Sarah brushed her thick long black hair back from her face, as she turned her head to the viewer.

Captain Genesis, was surprised to see her, albeit nicely surprised. Since taking on a lot of her Father's tasks, he had seen her more and more and every time he saw her, he found himself noticing more and more things about her. Today it was her hair.

"Em, Sarah, have we heard anything to worry about from above".

"Nothing to worry about Captain! America is absolutely convinced it may be the Russians playing about and the Russians are convinced the Americans are playing about. Neither one of them want to be the first to make a move that might make the situation worst. Both camps are talking about sending subs down to look around".

"What about our friends from UFO unit?"

"Officer Stirwell-Twine is unhappy that their agents in the north were not able to corroborate her sighting of a UFO, although they continue to state that they saw a UFO a couple of days later than her claimed sighting. It is now being suggested by Stirwell-Twine that she saw the invaders land and the agents in the north must have seen the strange helicopter. Officer Stirwell-Twine is not going to let this go. I'll keep you informed, Captain".

ELEVEN

THE LOST VIGIL

Back in the log cabin, Liam had been awake most of the night trying to work out how to help Santa. He wondered whether it would be better if they simply kept out of things and let the situation resolve itself.

After all, what would have happened if they hadn't been visiting? What if he wasn't the E-Contact. It could be a trap. One thing was sure though, they mustn't use the people carrier for a while. At least, not for a few days whilst the police were looking for this strange helicopter reported in the paper.

So that morning it was decided that Liam and Brandon would go and make some subtle enquiries about Alfred Pike and Ernest Pratt, in the village and Beth & Luke could take the children skiing again.

The children were naturally delighted about this,

especially Jimmy and George who were desperate to try the snow boards.

When the group reached the village they parted as planned. By now, the children knew the drill and were soon on the ski slopes.

Jimmy and George were trying out the snow boards. They found a group of other children with snow boards and they were all encouraging each other to try different turns and jumps.

Snow and Tayla decided to stay with the skis and away from groups of children. Tayla was still conscious of the fact that she hadn't quite mastered the art of skiing and preferred to perfect her skills, whilst not being watched by too many strangers. So she chose to stay with Snow, who, she had to admit, was doing so much better than her.

On the other hand, Beth and Luke were constantly pulling each other up from being on their bottoms, quite oblivious of the others on the slopes.

The slopes were busy, as usual, and Snow and Tayla were soon joined by Alfie and Ernie whom they recognised from Santa's grotto as his helpers and who had helped teach them to ski the day before.

"Hi, Snow, shall I carry your bag for you. You might be able to turn better?" said Alfie, putting his hand under her shoulder strap, making ready to slip it off her shoulder.

"No, I must carry my bag" and, as she tugged away from him his hand slipped into her bag.

Alfie immediately let out a loud yell "What have you got in your bag? It just bit me".

"My friend only bites if he doesn't know you", Snow smiled defiantly.

Snow repositioned her bag. "How dare he!" she thought.

Tayla hadn't connected Alfie's yell to something in Snow's bag, which Snow was somewhat relieved about. Tayla had only seen Alfie slipping and sliding all over the ice after offering to take Snow's bag and had presumed he had lost his balance, but she could now see that Snow was a little upset.

"Snow, Alfie was only trying to help. Your bag is a bit larger today!"

"I've just put an extra jumper in there in case I get cold".

Beth and Luke were still helping each other up every now and again and the twins were being taught all kinds of movements on the snow boards by other kids on the slopes. So, the girls carried on skiing but it wasn't long before they were again joined by Alfie and Ernie.

Ernie had convinced Alfie that he was being a big baby and that he must have caught his hand on a zip or something like that. The elves also seemed to think that Snow's bag was larger than normal and therefore the present must be tucked in there.

Ernie decided that he would distract Tayla while Alfie grabbed the bag from Snow. After all, as he reassured Alfie, "we are expert skiers, once you have the bag we can just ski off and disappear. Once we have the money we don't have to return to the village".

The idea sounded good to Alfie so when he got close to Snow he grabbed her wrist to bring her closer but grabbed her wrist Vigil at the same time. As he did this, Snow twisted her wrist to get away from him and the strap broke, freeing Snow and leaving Alfie standing there with her wrist Vigil in his hand. "Oops".

He looked around, a little embarrassed, to see whether Ernie was watching but he was engrossed in showing Tayla a new turn. He threw the wrist Vigil on the ground and turned back to grab Snow again but, she was nowhere to be seen.

Snow had skied towards the trees. She was not going to let that elf have her little friend. Snow thought that if she could hide behind a tree she could look to see where the others were. She couldn't call them on her Vigil because that was now gone.

Snow kept skiing and skiing. Every time she looked back, she could see the elf not far behind her and so she kept skiing on and on, twisting and turning over the snow and around trees until, she suddenly found herself flying through the air on the ridge of a snow bank. And: then falling, falling and rolling and rolling until her little body slammed heavily against a tree stump in her path.

Alfie, the elf that had been following Snow saw her go over the ridge but didn't want to follow her any more. He thought it would be pointless to because Ernie his mate was still back on the slopes and wouldn't know where he was.

So Alfie returned to the slopes determined to act as if nothing had happened.

Meanwhile, Beth and Luke had been checking on the children and discovered that Tayla was panicking because she had lost sight of Snow. Tayla had not just lost sight of Snow but she had discovered Snow's Vigil, which was her only means of calling for help, and she was beginning to scream out her name.

Beth, without hesitation, pressed her Vigil to call for help from the Logan brothers. She knew that, with the evening drawing in, they all needed to try and find Snow as quickly as possible.

TWELVE

CAPTAIN GENESIS

Back on the Viridis 6000, Louis who was monitoring the children's health noticed the absence of Snow's heart-beat.

"Captain, something terrible might have happened to Snow. I've lost her heart beat".

The crew began to gather around the monitor, searching for any sign that might show that Snow was still alive.

"What about the other heart beats?" enquired the Captain.

"The pulses are very erratic, with a chemical imbalance implying that they are all nervous or anxious about something".

Captain called the Intelligence Unit and requested that Roger and Sarah Baker come to the bridge.

"Roger, can we get visual contact on the children?" pleading with them, the Captain, looked desperately backwards and forwards at Roger and his daughter Sarah.

"Captain, it depends where they are. If they are in a building, it might be possible to hear them. If they are outside, we might only be able to see them but we'll need to go back to our unit. I'll call you if we can get anything".

THIRTEEN

PILLO THE REINDEER

The Logan brothers had arrived on the slopes on jet skis, in response to Beth's Vigil contact and whilst Jimmy and George climbed on to the back of their jet skis, they had suggested that Luke get a jet ski with Beth. Tayla volunteered to say behind, in case Snow came back. And: if that was the case, she would be able to signal to them on her Vigil.

Of course, there were many reasons why Tayla volunteered to stay behind but, she was not able to tell the others at the moment. One reason was because she felt really guilty that she had let Snow out of her sight and she couldn't bear it, if they found her harmed. Another reason was that she had just caught sight of Alfie, the elf who had been teaching Snow to ski. She thought he might know where she was.

"No he said. She had this thing about her bag and she ran off".

"Well, why didn't you tell me straight away", she yelled at him, angrily pushing him to the ground as she stamped off towards a reindeer hitched to an unused sledge.

She put her arms around his neck and stroked his nose. She noticed that his name was Pillo as it had been printed on his reigns "Oh, Pillo I wish you could help me. We need to find Snow",

The reindeer nodded his head and stamped one of his feet, as if he would, if he could but......

"Don't worry, of course, you can't. We need to think of something else" and she leaned against him, for inspiration.

Meanwhile, the others on the jet skis had been going around and around. They had all been calling out. The light was failing and the slopes were now quite dark. Fortunately, the jet skis had lights on them and the children kept on looking.

FOURTEEN

CAPTAIN GENESIS

"Captain, do you want to look at this. The picture is very dark but, by using the co-ordinates of the pulses and heat detectors, we think we have found them. There appears to be six of them looking for something or someone".

Sarah continued "Tayla is not with them, she's over here" and swivelled the picture around to show Tayla with her arms around a reindeer.

"Any sign of Snow".

"No, oh, wait a minute, what's this. We'll get in closer. There she is. Her heat is not strong. That's what they're doing. They're looking for Snow and she has obviously lost her Vigil!"

But just as Sarah and the Captain began to sigh with relief, Sarah swivelled the picture back to the children and they realised how far away they were from her and in fact they were going in the wrong direction in their hunt for her.

"Oh dear" thought Captain Genesis "this was just what Beth and the Counsel feared. They knew Snow's communication and interaction skills with the animals would be immature and this was a situation in which they needed to be very mature and, with a desperate desire to motivate her, the Captain began to talk to her, as if she could hear him. "Snow you have to wake up. You have to start shouting. Start crying or something. Start crying for your Mother. Let the animals around you hear you!"

If ever there was a time when the Captain and his crew wished they could intervene in some way, this was it but, there was absolutely nothing they could do.

FIFTEEN

A BIG HUG FOR THE DOE

Snow began to stir. She had no idea where she was. It was dark and she was very cold and frightened. She felt a little movement in her bag underneath her and realised she was possibly quashing Lemmie.

"Oh Lemmie, I'm sorry but I couldn't let him have you". She put her hand into the bag and could feel that Lemmie was very cold and was concerned that he had been hurt. It was a large bag, much too big for her really but her Mum had made it.

It had different colours and patterns sewn on it with various sized tassels running off the edges. As she ran her fingers over the different textures she mumbled to herself "Oh Mum, what shall I do and in desperation, she let out a loud cry "Mum, oh! Mum" and curled up on the tree trunk clutching her bag closely to her and sobbing.

Unbeknown to Snow, a Mother had heard her. A doe, a Mother deer, had heard her cry and had come to find her. She sensed that Snow was getting cold and was expressing a childlike fear, so she lay down close to her, providing a little warmth and shelter from the dark cold air. Snow was so relieved to see her that she crawled on her knees and threw her arms around her neck "Thank you, thank you".

Snow wanted to sleep but the doe kept making a bleating sound every now and again keeping her awake. This reassured her that she was no longer alone.

Meanwhile, the reindeer that Tayla had begun talking to, began to get agitated and the driver wanted Tayla to leave the reindeer alone, saying that he needed to be resting. Then, contrary to the driver's intentions, the reindeer began to trot off down the path and Tayla hopped quickly on the back of the sleigh.

The sleigh driver kept instructing the reindeer to stop but he continued on and on. The pathway wove along a narrow tree lined avenue. She could see some lights coming from the village below her but above her on the other side of the lane were dense trees and heavy snow.

Suddenly, coming down from the mountain towards the lane, Tayla could see the others on their jet skis. They were about to head back to the ski reception area, when they caught sight of Tayla. She waved to them, indicating that they were to follow her. She didn't know exactly why because she wasn't sure what the reindeer had heard but she had convinced herself that the reindeer must have heard Snow's cries.

Once Tayla was sure the others were following, she climbed into the front with the driver who by now had given up, trying to turn the reindeer around. "I'm sorry young lady but we'll just have to see what he wants. He's a strange one this one, certainly tonight".

The reindeer went on and on until he suddenly came to a stop. Tayla jumped down from the sleigh and went to him. "What can you hear Pillo?"

Tayla listened and to the right of her, up into the trees she could hear the bleating sound of a doe. "She's got Snow" shouted Tayla. "Please wait", she said to the driver, as she began to walk up towards the trees.

The jet skis followed and gave light to her path and it wasn't long before she saw the doe resting beneath the tree with Snow curled up between her limbs.

The Viriddion visitors were all giving the doe very large hugs and thanking her for looking after Snow. Once the reindeer's driver had given them a lift back to their log cabin, Beth gave him a gift of money to get Pillo extra carrots and apples.

That evening the children had a lot to talk about. All of them were so pleased to have Snow back with them and Snow should have been happy that she was back safely with her family but she knew she would have to tell them, sooner or later, about Lemmie.

The Logan brothers also had a lot to tell Beth and Luke about their day in the village but decided to keep it for another day.

The log cabin soon fell very quiet as the children fell asleep one by one. During their sleep each one of them found themselves re-living the anxious searching time for Snow on the slopes. And: Snow found herself back on the slope, being chased, rolling and rolling, cuddling up with the doe, listening to her heart beat and .... "Oh no, Beth, Beth help", screamed Snow, sitting bolt upright.

"It's all right Snow, you're just dreaming".

"Beth, the doe is not well. I heard her talk to me. She said, she was tired and that it was time to go".

"Snow, you are really tired yourself. You must sleep and we will talk this through in the morning and, in fact, we will need to talk about a lot of things in the morning, won't we Snow?"

Beth gave Snow a motherly kiss on the forehead and laid her gently back down. Snow settled, cradling her bag as usual.

SIXTEEN

OFFICER GWENDOLINE STIRWELL-TWINE

Newly wed, Gwendoline Stirwell-Twine in the American UFO office was having none of it. How dare her boss and colleagues make light of her claim to have seen a UFO on her honeymoon evening. She knew what she saw and somehow she was going to prove it.

As Gwendoline kept on reminding her new husband, while she anxiously shovelled the saucepans around on the stove and prepared supper, "I spent years in a home being told to be seen and not heard, so I've not spent years studying terrestrial life and flying objects, just to be silenced and simply told to forget what I saw".

"Yes dear. Look, why don't you have a break from that office and come with me. I've got to go to Lapland again and try and get an update on that story and a picture of that Santa. Apparently, lots of children wrote into the paper, after my sensational story about the Santa who robbed a bank in front of his elves, saying that they didn't believe my story and that I mustn't write stories like that. I ask you, some kids! Some even wrote and told the editor to sack me".

"Well a story like that at Christmas time, is probably not what kids want to hear. Some are worried about whether Santa will be able to deliver his presents, as usual. You would have thought that they'd have at least, given him bail. You know, so he could do his usual delivery on Christmas Eve".

"Oh, Gwendoline love, you really do need a holiday. Perhaps we could go skiing!"

SEVENTEEN

INSPECTOR MOODY

Back at the Lapland village police station, Inspector Moody was also having some nasty letters from children. He was being offered children's pocket money, to set Santa free and he and his officers were being called all the names under the sun. However, it wasn't so much the letters he was receiving or the content but, the amount he was receiving. He had to employ extra staff just to open the letters and he was beginning to think that, perhaps, he should have dealt with this incident in a different way, or he should have stopped the reporter from taking a photo that day.

His officers were also getting fed up with children calling into the Station, asking to see Santa to give him their Christmas list. So when Inspector Moody received a call from the newspaper for an update on the case, he was definitely not in a good mood. And, when asked about what evidence he had or what message he wished to give to the children of the world, he exploded with anger and threatened to put the next reporter, who telephoned or visited, into the cells with Santa.

EIGHTEEN

POLICE INSPECTION OF LOG CABIN

Meanwhile, the Viriddion visitors in the log cabin were deciding what to do next. Beth had spent some time with Snow, explaining how she may have heard what the doe was telling her and reassured her that, the doe did not appear to be suffering in any way and was therefore probably comforted by finding Snow at that time.

Beth continued to reassure Snow that, if it was the doe's time to die, she felt sure a game keeper would be keeping an eye open for her because game keepers and people that work with animals, have a great ability to understand an animal's health status and general wellbeing.

Snow wasn't that convinced that they shouldn't be off looking for the doe but, she knew Beth needed to meet

Lemmie. So slowly opening her bag, she smiled at the little face that came up to meet her with its big round black eyes. His little ears twitched and as his eyes opened and closed a couple of times, he moved his head a little from side to side and, on seeing the others in the room he quickly popped his head back down in the bag. Snow offered up the bag to Beth but, right at that moment, there was a knock at the door and Beth went off to answer it.

"Can I help you?" said Beth as she faced two police officers at the door.

"We're just doing the rounds Miss. We need to know whether you can tell us anything that might help us in our investigation into the bank robbery in the village a few days ago".

"No, I don't think so" answered Beth but seeing the snow falling heavily outside, thought they looked tired and cold. Also noticing that they were trying to peer into the log cabin towards the children's voices, she asked them in and offered them a cup of tea.

Beth introduced them to Luke and the children and as she poured them out a mug of tea, the children asked them questions like: what was it like to be a Policeman? Jimmy and George insisted on trying on their hats.

The officers asked them a lot of questions, especially about who they were and where they were from. Snow as usual was keen to quickly answer the questions.

"We're from Viridis and we have come to see some animals", she said, proudly looking around at the others.

Beth froze on the spot. She couldn't believe what she had just heard.

Beth knew this time would come when they could be

asked such questions about where they've come from and she knew the only answer from the children would be truthful but she hadn't really thought about how they would deal with it. She looked to Luke for possible inspiration and realised that he was looking at her probably hoping for the same.

"Oh, where's that then? I never was that good at geography?" smiled the taller policeman looking back at Snow.

"Miles and miles and miles away", replied Snow pointing to the ceiling.

"Luke and I are the children's teachers. The children are orphans and we have brought them on holiday. Would you like another cup of tea officers?" quickly trying to distract them in the hope the questions would stop.

To Beth's relief, the officers declined but then asked the children why they hadn't asked them anything about Santa. Snow said that it was because they knew the police would soon catch the baddies and set Santa free.

Astounded at the little girl's confidence, the officer said "Isn't it just possible that this Santa is bad".

"No", responded Snow angrily, "he gave me a present".

"Oh, what was that then?"

Snow quickly looked around to the other children "You know I can't open it until Christmas Day".

"Of course, of course", replied the officer as he nudged his colleague with a grin.

"Can we look in your garage? Sorry, just routine. We need to make sure you're not hiding a strange looking helicopter in there" and laughed.

Luke went out and opened the garage door.

"Cor, what a super carrier! What make is that?"

"It's a Viridis Multi Transporter".

"Purpose built I presume. Bet that cost something. No doubt belongs to the school. Well, I think we can cross this garage off the list; this is definitely not a helicopter. Ben, come and look at this".

However, he could see that Ben, his colleague, was far too busy to look and that he would have to take his word that the garage didn't have a helicopter in it. His colleague was talking to Tayla in an attempt to get as much information but her response was to shyly tilt her head towards the ground where she was moving the snow around her feet. As she swayed, her long red-flamed hair hung across one side of her face. She was saying nothing.

"Luke, when are you going back home?"

"Oh we've got about another week yet. The children want to go to the zoo and I think they've got attached to the ski slopes".

"You said your drivers were also staying with you: are they around?"

"You'll probably find them in the village or on the ski slopes".

"Well, have a nice holiday kids and thanks for the tea".

The officers' left and the children settled. Beth and Luke had decided that, after the fright Snow gave them the day before, they ought to spend a day in the warm, especially as the snow had been falling heavily again.

The Logan brothers had decided earlier to go to the village and said that they would bring supper back with them. So a bath and hair night for the children is was.

NINETEEN

ALFIE AND ERNIE

Whilst the girls washed and dried each other's hair and Luke and the twins chatted quietly completing their diaries for the past couple of days, their log cabin was the centre of attention for two off duty elves who were on their way home after working with the temporary Santa, The original Santa was of course still being held at the Police Station in the village.

"Are you sure she hasn't opened the present yet?"

"Sure I'm sure. They would have handed it into the Police Station by now, wouldn't they!"

"I wouldn't have. Give us a leg up and let me look into that window".

"But Ernie, we've already looked through the cabin and it wasn't there"

"Right, so she must have had it on her ....erk

......", Ernie lost his footing in the snow beneath the girls' bedroom window and Alfie, somersaulted and landed face down in the snow.

When the elves finally got it together, Alfie peered around the room. It was dark outside, so with the light on in the bedroom, Alfie was able to have a good look around the room, knowing that he would probably not be seen, if he kept low.

Alfie could see Beth brushing her long brown hair in the corner and Tayla brushing Snow's wavy sliver blonde hair, while she sat on one of the beds. Then he spotted her bag and ......it was moving.......

"I told you Ernie, she's got an animal in her bag. Look, you come up and see".

After some slipping and sliding, they changed places and Ernie peered through the window.

"No, you hip hop, whatever she's got in there it's just sliding backwards and forwards to the movement of the little one as she bounces on the bed", and as he said that, a small part of her white jumper shot out of the top of the bag.

"No, it's not an animal; it's definitely the money bag. She has opened the box and stuffed the sack into her bag to open later. We've got to get it". That decision came with a sudden movement and they both ended up rolling about in the snow again.

The elves hung around the cabin trying to decide what to do. Then they heard the Logan brothers arrive back and the light went out in the bedroom. Beth called the girls into another room to have their supper.

"Now you lift me up and I'll get the window open and

then I'll lift you up and you can nip in and get the bag while Snow's in the other room".

"Why me? It's always me!"

"Stop moaning, somebody clever has to look out".

The plan went very well. The window was opened, the elves changed positions and Alfie slipped in the bedroom. The room was very dark, so all he could do was feel on the bed for the bag but the bag wasn't there.

"Oh, drat, she's taken it with her".

Alfie leaned out of the window for instructions from Ernie but Ernie was gone. "Now what am I going to do", he moaned.

He sat back in the room. "At least it's warm in here", he thought.

Alfie kept popping his head out the window to check for Ernie but, he couldn't see him anywhere. Just then he heard sounds outside the bedroom door and he quickly managed to crawl underneath a bed just as the light was being switched on.

"Brr, it's cold in here", shivered Beth and noticing the window open, she closed it, locked it and took the key with her to ensure the girls didn't leave it unlocked again, especially with burglars about she thought.

One by one the girls came back to their room and settled in their beds for the night and the log cabin again became silent while the children slept.

Ernie, who was waiting outside was so cold that he couldn't hang around any longer and made his way back to their cottage in the village.

Alfie slowly crawled out from under the bed. He

noticed the window was closed and locked, so he thought he would have to leave the cabin by the front door but first he needed the bag.

He crawled around the bedroom floor very quietly looking for the bed which Snow was in and having found it, he studied it for her bag but he couldn't see it. Alfie then saw a shape under the covers and guessed that it was the bag. Then, he noticed the strap of the bag was hanging down the side of the bed, he very slowly and gently pulled the strap and slipped the bag out from under the covers.

"At last. The trouble I've gone through to get this bag. Ernie's going to have to sing for it, for abandoning me", he thought as he made his way to the bedroom door and out into the sitting area. He noted that the other doors in the cabin were closed and he continued to creep slowly to the front door.

He went to open the front door but it was stiff and as he wanted to do it really quietly he decided that he would need two hands to do the task. He first attempted to put the strap over his head and hang the bag across his shoulder like Snow carried it but, then thought it looked girlie. So, seeing a chair close by, laid the bag down on it. He pulled and pulled the door and it finally opened.

He stepped out on to the front step to check that the coast was all clear but, just at that moment, Liam and Brandon who had been working on the transporter opened the inner door from the garage to the sitting area of the cabin and as this door opened into the sitting area it knocked against the front door slamming it shut, shutting Alfie out in the snow.

"Hey, who didn't shut the front door properly? We'll

need to remind them about that in the morning, especially with burglars about".

It wasn't long after Liam and Brandon had turned the sofas in the sitting area into beds and had settled down for the night that Snow stirred and couldn't feel her bag close to her. She must have left it in the sitting area she thought and, sure enough, she found it but Lemmie was not inside. She quickly and quietly crawled about on the sitting area floor but couldn't find him and so she returned to her bed to have another look, only to find that he had tucked himself right down to the bottom of her bed. "That's strange Lemmie, you don't normally go downwards".

TWENTY

CAPTAIN GENESIS

Back on the Viridis 6000, Captain Genesis was concerned about the Slender Loris which Snow had in her bag and called the acting Head of the Animal Communication and Inter-actionism Unit to the bridge.

Captain Genesis wanted to know how dangerous the Slender Loris could be and what problems Beth could expect to have. Julie explained that Lemmie looks like a type of Slender Loris, only it was a miniature type being smaller than the Dwarf Slender Loris found on Earth, and that this Slender Loris grows no larger than a size of a man's hand.

Julie continued to explain that Lemmie, which was the name the Unit had given him, could easily be kept alive on fruit and odd bits of food that Snow would normally eat. According to college records, the Earth has not discovered a miniature Slender Loris, similar to the species that lived on Viridis and that, Lemmie, may bite a stranger but it would only be a nip and certainly not deadly or poisonous, contrary to the type of Slender Loris found on Earth or at least up until now.

"So no problem then!" sighed Captain Genesis.

"Well not exactly Captain. Unfortunately, the whole group would be in big trouble if the authorities discovered Lemmie. You see, to them, Lemmie is a recognisable Slender Loris and a Slender Loris is an endangered species on the Earth and any person found in possession of a Slender Loris could be fined, even imprisoned".

"Oh, great: as if they haven't got enough on their plate at the moment".

"Captain, an American sub is in our range".

Captain Genesis moved over to the monitor Louis was watching. He thought it had been too quiet from above but he had been unable to decide what to do, if a sub discovered them. He noted that although the American sub was within their range, they were still a few miles outside the subs range and called Roger in Intelligence.

"Roger, have you picked the sub up and can you tell me what they are saying or possibly thinking".

"Apparently, they are trying to treat this as a normal routine, so as not to cause friction with the Russians. They're extending their area of search north/west which could be a problem for us".

"Louis, what room have we got to our north/west?"

"We could possibly squeeze a little further under the ice ridge but it would mean we would have to take the ship deeper. We have not taken the ship as deep before,

Captain. I'm not sure how the pressure of water and ice above us would affect the infrastructure!"

The Captain sat silent for some time as he watched the radar screen. He knew that if he left now, with the Russian and American ships so close, they would surely see them, and they would never be able to return to the Earth again safely because Earth's military forces would be waiting for them.

Just at that time, Old Ridoros appeared on the bridge. He could see what was going on and as if he could read his grandson's thoughts, he took the Captain's left hand with his left hand, lifted it up, and placed it across his own chest in the Viridis position, as a sign of strength and respect. In doing so, he then placed his old worn right hand over the Captain's.

"You must not think of the children. The children will be safe or as safe as any person now residing on Earth. Your duty is to the Viriddions' on this ship, just as the children and other Viriddions' now on Earth will know their duty - a duty to take care of the animals and protect them from the Yapikus and extinction".

Old Ridoros rested down in the Captain's chair, whilst his grandson walked around checking on various monitors. He had put on a strong show for his grandson but, in reality he was rather hoping they could stay put and not have to leave. He began to think back to when he first set foot in a Viriddion Spaceship. That was the day when ....His thoughts were suddenly interrupted by Louis informing the Captain that he needed to make up his mind because the sub was nearing the point at which it would be able to detect the Viridis 6000.

"We have no choice. We need to go a little deeper and try to move under the ice ridge a little further. To leave Earth or stay here could put the crew at risk. Prepare crew and proceed at slow-stop speed or our movement might be detected!"

The bridge, on the Viridis 6000 became very tense and busy, as the crew prepared for a change of position under the ice ridge in the Arctic.

TWENTY-ONE

OFFICER GWENDOLINE STIRWELL-TWINE AND HUSBAND WINSTON -V- INSPECTOR MOODY

Meanwhile, the freelance reporter Winston Stirwell and his new wife Gwendoline arrived in Lapland to obtain an up-to-date report on the Santa who was being held for breaking into a village bank.

Inspector Moody was not exactly pleased to see them, especially as the local children had taken up a demonstration outside the Police Station, chanting: "Set Santa Free - Sack the Reporter. Set Santa Free. Sack the Reporter".

"I told you, not to enquire again. There is nothing I can tell you. Santa's claiming he's innocent and his lawyers have visited him. That's all I can tell you at the moment.

You need to keep yourself hidden. If the kids out there discover who you are, they're likely to bury you alive in snow!"

"Winston only reported what he saw happening", butted in Gwendoline sympathetically slipping her hand in Winston's.

"That's not the way the kids of the world see it. You had better leave by the back door".

"Can't I just get a picture of Santa in the cell?" insisted Winston.

"Get out, before I lock you in a cell", growled Inspector Moody and shoved them both out the back door, which sent them slipping and sliding along the path.

Inspector Moody was getting physically and mentally exhausted. The kid's campaign was keeping him in the office, day and night for extra security. His boss at Head Quarters had suggested that he was not trying hard enough to find the stolen money, even though he had extra men out there looking for it.

He had even brought in the two elf workers, who had originally claimed that they saw a man looking like Santa breaking into the Bank, for an identification parade. He had secretly hoped that they would not point Santa out from a line-up of Santa's but, they had. So he had no option but to hold him.

He had even called Santa's lawyers because they had not visited him since that earlier visit. He was concerned that as Santa had named the elf workers, as Alfred Pike and Ernest Pratt in the interview with them, they should at least be looking deeper into that story.

All Santa's lawyers had said was that a defence was

being prepared. And, to top it all, his wife was on the phone every day nagging him to come home or she would lock him out for good.

"Officers, make sure those two don't return" he ordered watching the two hanging onto each other as they walked off.

Of course, Winston was not at all put off. He was used to having to fight for stories. He considered he was doing the public a favour, if there was a dishonest Santa out there.

And: Gwendoline, well she was just happy to be away from the Intelligence Office for a while and on another winter break with her new husband. She loved looking around the village shops and the clothes stores. Back home everything seemed so busy but, she felt relaxed here and not under pressure to prove she was good at her job. Although, she knew she mustn't relax too much to the point that she would forget about the UFO she saw on her honeymoon in Scotland.

"Oh hi, are you on holiday here too" Gwendoline excitedly asked as she caught sight of the children with Beth and Luke. They were looking in a shop window displaying many different patterns of material.

"Yes, we went to visit Santa", said Snow running forward to take Gwendoline's hand, as if she had known her for years.

Gwendoline took the little gloved hand into hers and looked into the window with her. "What lovely material. I can just see you in a dress made of that one".

Tayla immediately joined in. "Ooh yes, and I would love one made in that material", pointing to shimmering pink velour. "I have only seen such pretty materials in books".

"Yes, I understand. When I was in an orphanage I only had clothes passed down to me. I don't suppose things have changed that much today!"

The boys as usual were busy throwing snow missiles at each other and definitely not at all interested in a shop window displaying girlie materials, until they caught sight of the shop window with model ships and aeroplanes. "Cor, Jimmy look at these".

Luke saw Winston wander over and join the boys as they got excited about the models in the window, and he was concerned.

Luke had felt a little uneasy about the couple, when they first met in Scotland but, he thought he was being over protective. He thought the lady was overly chatty as if she was trying to get personal information from them and the man was overly quiet, as if he was hiding something.

He had intended to talk to Beth about his thoughts but, since leaving Scotland, he had almost forgotten about them. He looked over at Beth who looked back at him and he knew that they were thinking alike.

"What do you think of Santa in prison, then boys", questioned Winston.

The boys looked at each other and laughed and continued to point out particular models in the window.

"Fancy poor old Santa being kept in prison, I hope they let him out before Christmas or you won't get a present from him, Snow!" smiled Gwendoline.

"It doesn't matter because he has already given me his present, although I might give it back".

"Why, what is it".

"Of course, I haven't opened it yet. If he's bad then he's not really Santa and I'll give it back".

Gwendoline couldn't believe how honest the little girl was. She was certain that she wouldn't have returned any present she received, however or whoever gave it to her.

"Have you been skiing Snow".

"Yes but we have to be careful because there are some strange looking people that chase you and you might get lost, like I did".

"Oh dear, what did they look like" quizzed Gwendoline.

"They had big ears with a pointed hat and one was little like me and he tried to take my bag".

"Gosh, that sounds frightening. You must stick close to your teachers" replied Gwendoline looking over at Beth and Luke with a smile.

Just then Liam and Brandon arrived on jet skis and offered the children a lift up to the ski slopes. Jimmy jumped on the back of Liam and George on the back of Brandon and the Logan brothers said they would return for the girls.

With the girls gone too, Winston and Gwendoline went to find a café. Beth and Luke strolled up to the slopes on their own.

For the first five minutes Beth and Luke just walked in silence. This was the first time that they had been alone without the children around and the absence for both of them was quite clearly a time to relax and they did not appear to be in any hurry to get to their destination.

Beth slipped her arm in his arm, seeking support for

safe walking and Luke willingly made his arm available. They found themselves chatting about the situation they were in with Santa and wondered how things were going on back on the ship with Captain Genesis.

They reminded each other about their strict instructions not to return to the ship until they had collected the data on particular animals and information on a particular E-Contact who was supposed to be based in Finland but with whom the ship had lost contact.

Beth and Luke also discussed their concerns in relation to Snow's innocent and honest answers, which could get them into trouble if they weren't careful, and Luke let Beth know about the odd feelings, he was getting about Winston and Gwendoline.

"It's odd Beth, how they always seem to be asking questions. It's as if they constantly want to know about us but they haven't told us a thing about themselves or why they are here. I thought they had just had a holiday".

"Maybe they're government agents and they're getting ready to pounce on us" laughed Beth, giving Luke a little push, as if to make him jump. On doing so, she slipped a little and Luke had to put both arms around her to stop her falling over.

He held her close and he sensed that she was comforted from their closeness. However, it was at times like this, when he found himself with a warm happy feeling inside, that he suddenly remembered the loss of his parents during the virus, his younger brother Mikey he had left behind on Viridis 6000 and so began to feel guilty for feeling a little happy.

He began to wonder how Mikey and the other young

student pilots were coping. Mikey was eighteen and hoping to pilot a Viridis Multi-Transporter but because of the loss of crew members and with Liam and Brandon away from the ship, this might now be difficult for him.

Beth sensed Luke's thoughtfulness and it reminded her that Luke, like all of them, needed time to reflect upon the family they had lost and or left behind on the ship.

When Luke realised he had been deep in thought, he apologised. But, Beth reassured him by taking his left hand in her right and saying "It's all right, I know where you were and I was there with you!"

Beth and Luke spent the rest of the day skiing, or trying to ski with the children. Snow and Tayla were always determined to get their movements perfect and Jimmy and George were trying to complicate the movements by switching on their wrist Vigils to play one to one no-contact tag with each other.

The next day soon came and when Beth awoke that morning she noticed the weather looked brighter and decided that they needed to get on and visit the local zoo to collect some data from a tiger.

As Beth began to think of the tasks before them, she smiled to herself, as she remembered being very young about four or five, sitting on a bench with other children in the ships field, and her Grandfather Ridoros telling them the Viridis story.

Beth knew the Viridis story; of course, it had been passed on from one generation to the next and no doubt slightly exaggerated over time. Perhaps the story told by her Grandfather was one of those he told about a man with large wings who appeared in the Viridis sky and said to the Viriddion people, "You are very sad people because you do not have any animals on your planet. I will send some animals for you to love and look after and this will make you happy. If, when I return they have all died or you are not caring for them, I will remove them and you will become very unhappy people again".

"Beth, are we really going to the Zoo today", Snow said excitedly interrupting Beth's warm nostalgic thoughts. "Beth, I really need to show you what I have in my bag. He just hopped in when I wasn't looking and then it was too late. I'm so sorry".

Beth looked curiously at Snow who was clearly uneasy. Snow was no relation to Beth but since leaving the ship, she felt more like a mother than a teacher to her. To see Snow unhappy caused Beth to be unhappy and so, desperately wanting to help her, she knelt down and peeped into Snow's bag to see two very large eyes looking back at her.

"Oh Snow". She wanted to be angry but, how could she? She had not held a little creature, such as this, in her hands for many years and she knew the wonderful feelings Snow must have been experiencing, whilst caring for it. "Has his little leg healed?" she said as she saw the splint and bandage on his leg.

Snow carefully raised Lemmie from the cosy comforts of her bag and gently handed him to Beth, who cradled him in both her hands.

Beth felt Lemmie's tiny limbs and finger tips as he made attempts to push against her palms and raise his head up between her cupped hands to see his new handler. Beth experienced the warm intense love for him that only an animal lover could experience.

She felt his strong limbs and observed how well he was. Beth gently took the splint off the leg and congratulated Snow for looking after him so well who was then bombarded by many questions.

"Where did he come from?" "What's his name?" "What have you been feeding him on?" "Is he hurting" "Oh Snow what have you done!"

Tayla and the boys all wanted to take turns in holding him but the Logan boys were not as excited. "How can we keep this from the authorities?"

TWENTY-TWO

INFECTED SHEEP

It wasn't long afterwards, that whilst the Viriddion visitors climbed into the carrier to make their way to the Zoo, a couple of off duty elves were also making ready to follow the family to where ever they were visiting today.

Alfred and Ernest were parked just a short distance away up the lane from the children's cabin. They were getting very anxious because they had not intended to stay so long in their jobs as elf workers.

They were also frustrated because they were absolutely convinced that the bag of money they had stolen from the bank was hidden in the present which had then been given by Santa to Snow. They thought she had chosen to keep the present until Christmas Day in her bag: The one that she always seemed to carry around with her. The one they just couldn't get hold of.

"Don't worry Ernie, that bag has been so close, we will get it today, without fail".

"We must stick to them like glue. Whatever they do, we do. Just keep a short distance back so they don't see us.

The Viriddion carrier wound around the lanes, onto large motorways and back into small lanes again and whilst the children pointed out farm animals in the fields and different coloured cars and lorries on the roads, Liam and Brandon were busy discussing why an old looking white Ford Popular car should be following them.

"Yes Brandon, I agree it looks as if we're being followed but it could just be somebody staying in our village who happens to be visiting the same Zoo as us on the same day as us. Just keep an eye on it".

"It could be that reporter and his wife? Did any of you kids tell them that we were going to the Zoo today?"

Mutters of "No", "No" came from behind him and, although Liam wasn't exactly convinced with that answer he had noticed that the children were unusually quiet and decided not to press them anymore.

Beth had also noticed how quiet the children were but thought they might be just a little tired from being out in the Earth atmosphere so much, over these past few days.

However, Beth became more and more concerned when Jimmy and George both put one of their hands over their mouths and the other hand across their stomachs and began groaning as if they were going to be sick.

"Stop Liam, the boys need fresh air".

Liam pulled into an access area to a Farm. A large wooden double gate prevented the carrier from going too far into the drive and as soon as the carrier stopped the children piled out.

Jimmy and George carried on crouching over, as if they were in pain with their hands over their mouths and groaning "The sheep: the sheep, they're in pain".

While Luke tried to settle the boys on a grass bank, Beth and the girls climbed up onto the large gate to see an unmade drive leading up into a wooded area with large fields laying either side of it.

The fields were full of sheep. Some were in groups, some lying down and some on their own and Beth noticed that one was quite close to the gate but not close enough for her to touch.

"Liam can you see a farm house or farmer anywhere?"

The Logan boys got their binoculars out and after looking over hedges on either side of the lane, they said they could see nothing and presumed the house must be quite a way up the lane.

"Luke, I'm going to have to go over the gate with the girls. Keep an eye on the boys".

After Liam had given Beth and Snow a hand over the gate and Brandon had helped Tayla, the girls slowly approached one of the sheep that was lying close to the field hedge alongside the lane.

They laid their hands on the sheep to comfort and reassure it and observed that it had sticky eyes and its breathing was laboured, suggesting an infection. Then Beth noticed some jagged torn skin blood marks on his back.

"She's been bitten", exclaimed Beth with a fear in her voice.

"What by?" said Tayla, Snow and all the others simultaneously behind the hedge.

"Is it a fox or a dog?" suggested Tayla.

"I'm guessing because I have only seen these marks in a book before but these, with an infection accompanied with abdominal pain that Jimmy and George are experiencing can only be that the Yapikus have visited this field!"

At the word "Yapikus", Luke was opening up the floor of the carrier and retrieving a selection of vials, needles and containers. Luke knew exactly what a Yapikus can do.

His Father had placed a scene following a Yapikus invasion on Viridis, on his Visionars and he therefore knew the speed in which they would have to work to save the flock because if the Yapikus had attacked this sheep it would have attacked the rest of the sheep in the field.

Within seconds Luke was retrieving samples of blood from the sheep. Beth prepared the correct antidote compound. Once done, she administered it and watched as the sheep slowly got to its feet.

Beth explained to Snow and Tayla that the sheep would now be the nurse-carrier of the antidote to the other sheep but it would need to go and rub itself against the other sheep in the fields, so that they too could receive the benefit of the antidote.

Tayla drew the sheep close to her and talked quietly to her and within minutes the sheep was walking off across the field to the other sheep and Jimmy and George's abdominal pains slowly disappeared.

TWENTY-THREE

ALFIE AND ERNIE

Meanwhile, some way back up the lanes, the off duty elves were in a spot of bother. Their car had a puncture and they had scrambled about trying to put the spare tyre on. As usual, their pattern of work was not straightforward and it took a little time to accomplish.

When Alfie and Ernie did get driving again, they had lost sight of the children's carrier completely.

"Now what? We're stuck in the middle of nowhere, not knowing where we are meant to be going. Whose brilliant idea was this?" hissed Alfie, glaring at Ernie.

"Oh stop moaning. They haven't passed us, so they must be down here somewhere. Look, a sign to the Zoo. That's it; they're taking the children to the Zoo. So to the Zoo we shall go".

"The Zoo, oh great I haven't been to a Zoo to see the monkeys since I was a child!"

However, unbeknown to the off duty elves, the Viriddion visitors who had originally planned a day at the Zoo had seen a signpost back to the Lapland village, and made a unanimous decision to go to the Zoo another day, after the morning they had just had at the farm.

Although Jimmy and George were no longer in pain, they were very tired and Beth and Luke considered that they needed to explain all about the Yapikus to the children and how they treated any infection from an attack.

TWENTY-FOUR

CAPTAIN GENESIS

Back on Viridis 6000, Captain Genesis and his crew had manoeuvred the ship a little deeper into the Arctic Ocean, and further under an ice ridge. And: to their relief, the American sub had given up and moved away.

This had given Captain Genesis time to think about the other sighting of a UFO that the UFO unit had spoken about. He knew that if the Viriddions' had visited Earth then other visitors must have too, just as Viridis had been visited by space explorers. However, this thought alone did not unduly concern him, as it was the thought that not all visitors or explorers would be friendly, as Viridis had learnt to its detriment.

"Roger, have you anything further on the second sighting of a UFO?"

"It appears that it has landed a little further to the

103

South/West and on an island of ice. Several American ships have surrounded it and they are trying to communicate with it. Their Intelligence Unit has been speaking to the American President who wants to communicate to the Earth people that he wants to take a friendly approach towards explorers from the universe".

"Interesting! What has our E-Contact have to say?"

"He's been trying to put forward the argument that it would not be wise to assume that all explorers or space visitors will be friendly and that, just giving them the room to leave safely, may be the better option, especially if you don't know their intentions".

"Good advice. Can we get sight of this visiting ship?"

Roger brought up the view of the ship and they were instantly able to recognise it as a Yapikus craft. Captain Genesis had been told and warned by his Grandfather about the Yapikus and their gruesome way of manufacturing animal fur for trade.

He told Roger to call him if he heard anything new. Meanwhile, he was going to rest back with his Visionars to refresh his memory and even learn a little more about the Yapikus. As he rested back, he thought, "Well, at least the pressure is off us at the moment".

TWENTY-FIVE

YAPIKUS

Snow and the others were somehow glad to be back in their log cabin. They had called into a village store on the way back and picked up supper. After supper Beth checked the medical supplies and explained why she had chosen that particular medication to counteract the infection in the sheep.

Luke explained how they were already prepared with various chemical compounds to use against a Yapikus attack but he wasn't aware that they were visiting Earth animals, at the present.

He continued to explain that, usually, the Yapikus ships visit different planets once or twice a year. That they are not piloted by men but are automated by a control ship miles away from the planet they are directed to. And, they will send several ships to different parts of the planet they are targeting to obtain different kinds of animal fur.

"I don't understand" said Jimmy "why are they not manned.

"Well, that way, if a ship is destroyed or crashes, no one gets injured".

"But how can they collect fur, if the ships are not manned?" queried George.

Luke went on to explain that each ship, once it has landed, sends out pods about a foot in diameter. Some pods are joined together with spacing rods so that they can be directed to particular areas. The pods are sent out at night, so to an onlooker they might look like a flock of geese or similar.

"How can electronic pods be harmful" asked Tayla.

The pods will land close to their chosen area of invasion, into long grass or cornfields. Once landed the pods open up and release tiny automatic buttons, no larger than a fly, into the fields or bush lands. Each little mechanical button will land on its targeted animal, tear off a small piece of its fur and return to its pod.

Once the pods are filled, they return to their ship still under the cover of darkness and then the ship leaves the Planet.

"I'm sorry Luke, I still can't quite work out why this should be so harmful to the animals or the inhabitants of Earth!" insisted Tayla.

"Well you saw the sheep today. If we hadn't have treated them so quickly, they would have all died with an infection".

Luke continued to explain that the mechanical flies are

continuously building up bacteria, which means as soon as an animal's skin is torn, it leaves the wound infected and fatal for the animals.

"Luke, how can little pieces of fur be of any value to the Yapikus?"

"The Yapikus have built up a trade by growing animal fur. They have discovered how to produce a type of man-made material, from cells, which if planted with one single animal hair root on it, will multiply and simulate the animal fur from which it was taken from".

"This may seem like a simple question Luke but, why don't they just capture the animals and skin them, if that is their trade?"

"According to the Viridis ancient stories and stories from other planets, the animals that produce such beautiful fur were becoming extinct. The Viriddions' loved their animals and encouraged the growth of rich habitation that the animals needed, but multiple herds were being removed by the Yapikus. This coincided with the move in the planet's outer quadrant towards the Viridis Sun, resulting in the surface drying up. The small number of animals remaining on Viridis became extinct, except for some of the species we managed to bring to Earth".

"Why, have we not come across the Yapikus before?" queried Brandon.

"Well, Viridis hasn't supported such animal life for thousands of years now and therefore the visits by the Yapikus ceased and the stories would have been forgotten if it was not for the library records and memories held in our Visionars. Some of the older Viriddions' would have been able to tell us about some of the encounters on other planets and Old Ridoros is one of those who was caught up in a Yapikus invasion on Paridis, Viridis's sister Planet", Luke said as he looked over to Beth, who was nodding her head in agreement.

"Right, come on children, I think a good night's rest is in order and perhaps we'll try again for the Zoo tomorrow".

TWENTY-SIX

OFFICER GWENDOLINE STIRWELL-TWINE AND HUSBAND WINSTON

Gwendoline and Winston were up early the following morning. Gwendoline had been in contact with her UFO office and had been told about the American President's decision to be patient and wait for the inhabitants of the Spaceship to come out, so that the Earth people could let them know how friendly their intentions were.

Winston had been in contact with his editor of the paper he writes for, begging him that he be released from the Santa in prison story and transferred to the Iceland Spaceship story.

Gwendoline looked out of their kitchen window and looked down at the crowd of children still demonstrating outside the village Police Station. Mrs Stirwell-Twine thought that a rented apartment right opposite the Police Station would be an ideal place to be staying, whilst her husband was covering the story of Santa but Mr Stirwell wasn't so sure.

She took her apron off and neatly folded it beside the sink, drew her chair out from under the table, ran her hands down the back of her skirt to ensure it didn't crease up under her and, sat down. She proudly looked over to her husband, who had already chopped off the top of his boiled egg and was dipping in a finger of bread with one of his hands whilst holding the paper in the other. She noticed how serious he looked. He never smiled these days but she knew why.

Gwendoline remembered when Winston first came to the orphanage; he was always smiling and laughed at everything. But, one worker kept smacking him and sending him to a corner, saying that if he was smiling and laughing he was up to no good. So he learnt to keep his feelings to himself.

"My office are being very nice to me now Winston. They say they need me back".

"Well I've got to stay put. How they expect me to stay hidden from that lot, right outside our window I've no idea! Maybe I should dress up as an elf; there seem to be a lot about!"

"Oh yes, then I would have to dress up too if you did Winston, as it would look funny if I didn't"

"I was only joking, my dear".

"Winston, I've convinced the office to let me stay with you and the Santa story. I am absolutely convinced that the Martians would already have left the spaceship in that strange helicopter that was seen near here. And, furthermore, I'm sure they are connected to the Bank break-in and Santa in prison".

"Oh, that's good dear. Can I have another cup of tea? Cor, trust Terry to get that story – unidentified infection reported in a family of tigers in India and all I get is a little picture of the children gathering outside the prison with a caption "No Sign of Santa being Free For Christmas?", that's bound to make me the friend of the children, I don't think".

"Never mind dear, at least we have some children as our friends. Let's go skiing today and maybe we can bump into them. I wouldn't mind knowing what present Santa gave little Snow. She might let me have a little peep".

TWENTY-SEVEN

ALFIE AND ERNIE

Meanwhile, Alfie and Ernie, the other two people who, not only wanted a peep but wanted to obtain the present given to Snow from Santa, were sprawled out across the seats in their car. Totally exhausted and fast asleep.

Apparently, unaware the Viriddion visitors had not visited the zoo; they had spent the day before, checking it out looking for the children. They had visited the Monkey House, Tiger Land, Polar Bear Den and every animal pen in the zoo. But, the children were nowhere to be seen.

Alfie was so convinced that they were in the Monkey House, at one time, that he found himself locked in because the Keeper didn't see him hiding behind a large bale of straw. So Ernie had to keep the monkeys occupied at one end of their house, while Alfie tried to pick the lock.

When that didn't work, Alfie had climbed up high

in the outside cage, putting up with visiting children laughing at him, as he swung about with one hand or one leg, keeping the monkeys occupied while Ernie tried to pick the lock.

When Alfie did get free, the zoo was closed and they then had to find a way out, without setting the alarms off. Having now stirred from their sleep they realised that if they didn't get a move on back to the Lapland village and back to work, they would lose their jobs, they became exceptionally angry with each other for wasting another day.

TWENTY-EIGHT

INFECTED TIGERS

The Viriddion visitors had intended to try and get to the zoo today but after reading a paper that the Logan brothers had picked up in the village earlier that morning and then after receiving a telephone call from the Scotland E-Contact on one of their mobile phones, they had changed their minds. In fact they were now several miles into their next journey making their way as quickly as their transporter could take them to India and then on to Africa.

India was where a family of Tigers had been spotted with an unidentified infection and Rubin, the Scotland E-Contact, had also informed them that since the report in the paper, a pride of lions had been spotted with an unidentified infection in Africa.

Beth and Luke knew that they had to get the correct antidote compound to the tigers and lions within the next six hours or they would pass the infection on to others in the National Parks. Of course, a normal journey over land and sea by plane would take any Earth person more than six hours from Lapland, so the Viriddion visitors had to make a decision as to the type of transport they would use.

Liam was not happy with the decision they had finally made but it was somehow inevitable. They had to transform the transporter into the helicopter and use the aero-boosters to travel at supersonic speed.

This type of travel would be extremely dangerous and would possibly cause all sorts of responses from local military as the helicopter passed over controlled air space but the Viriddions' felt they had no choice.

Liam wanted to leave the children behind but, as soon as he made the suggestion, he knew the response he would get from Beth because, as he reminded himself, the Viriddion Counsel had chosen Beth, Luke and the children as a team.

Naturally, Beth and Luke had also considered leaving the children behind but, as they thought through the task before them, they knew that they would not be able to save the animals without the communication support skills of the children.

They needed the twins to say exactly where the animals were that were hurting, particularly wild animals who when sick or hurting often stayed very silent so as not to be seen and become pray for other animals.

Likewise, they needed Tayla and Snow, who would be able to talk to the animals or call to the animals, especially the animals that had been left to live in the wild natural environment of the Safari Parks and not used to people getting close to them.

As a result, Liam and Brandon had decided to fly high and to come down in the Indian National Safari Park from the North. They would have preferred a mission like this to take place in the dark, but that wasn't going to be possible and it would be in the heat of the afternoon that they would arrive.

So the Viriddions began their journey and whilst Beth and Luke talked through the tasks ahead of them with the children, the Logan brothers were constantly on the lookout for company.

When they approached the northern ridge of the Safari Park the children began to see elephants and rhinos. Then as the black helicopter came down low over the Park, Jimmy and George were beginning to show signs of abdominal pains.

At that point, the helicopter dropped lower but the ground was covered in dense shrubbery, making a landing impossible. Liam didn't want to land too far away from the animals they needed to treat because that would not only lose time but could possibly put the children in danger from being seen by gamekeepers.

Liam you must hover and let us down, if you get any lower we may frighten the wildlife. The children released their doors and they rose up, revealing a rope for each one of them to descend on.

Beth, Luke, Tayla, Jimmy, George and Snow, did not hesitate. They put both feet into individual stirrups and held on to the ropes, which took them to the ground at some speed. Jimmy and George led them to an area of bush and pointed to the family of tigers huddled together.

The Viriddion visitors knew that they couldn't hang around. The gamekeepers would soon become aware of them and would use guns if necessary, to remove them from the Park. And, even if the gamekeepers allowed them to do their job, they had to move on to Kenya urgently, or they would be too late to save the lions.

The Viriddions' sat down quietly under a tree, a few yards away from the family of tigers, knowing that they could not simply approach them, as it would be far too dangerous. The tigress, two cubs and five other grown tigers, were obviously in distress. Their eyes were very sticky and the fur on the fully grown tigers was freshly torn and bleeding, as if they had been attacked by a bunch of wild dogs. Beth and Luke set out the equipment and medication they needed while Tayla began to sing quietly. It wasn't long before Snow joined in and very shortly, the tigress began trying to stand up.

As she tried to get to her feet, one of the cubs pushed underneath, as if it was trying to help its mother to stand. Staggering and falling she very slowly made her way to the Viriddions' and laid down between Jimmy and George, who were both rolled up in a ball still clearly in pain, against the tree and groaning.

Tayla and Snow quickly stroked the tigress to reassure her whilst Luke gently took a blood sample and Beth injected the tigress with the antidotal compound to treat its infection. Tayla talked to the tigress and encouraged her to go and lick the other tigers to make them well.

The medication worked quickly and, it wasn't long

after the tigress had moved around her family licking them, they had begun to stand up and groom each other.

Whilst the tigers were busy, one of the cubs bounded over to the children, thinking he had found some new friends. Jimmy and George's pains began to reside and they cuddled and had a romp around with the cub until Beth and Luke signalled the children to the ropes hanging down from the helicopter.

The Viriddions' quickly packed their things away, ran to the ropes, put their feet back in the stirrups, which drew them back up to the helicopter and as they swung their doors back down, they could see a couple of land rovers approaching with armed men inside but, the Logan brothers were not intending to hang around and the helicopter, within seconds sped off South towards Kenya in Africa.

TWENTY-NINE

CAPTAIN GENESIS

On Viridis 6000 Captain Genesis and Old Ridoros was busy watching the children's movements on the monitor controlled by Roger Baker and his daughter Sarah.

"What was so different about Sarah today?" Captain Genesis was thinking. He couldn't make up his mind but he wanted to keep looking at her. Every time she looked at him, he turned away quickly looking at the monitor because he didn't want her to notice that his mind was elsewhere and not on the job.

However, Old Ridoros had noticed. How could he not. His grandson had not taken his eyes of Sarah from the moment she entered the bridge with her Father. His grandson's mind was normally very focused on the task ahead. "Mind you", he thought "if I was a hundred years younger......"

"Ridoros, what do you think of this?" Roger moved the monitor around to focus on an object in the desert, not far from the Safari Park in Africa.

"Oh no, that's another Yapikus ship. I'm not surprised; they don't normally do things in a one-off fashion. Where are the children now?"

"They've just left India. At the speed Liam's travelling, they'll reach Kenya in another hour".

"Have the authorities, anywhere, spotted the children?" enquired Captain Genesis daring to lift his eyes towards Sarah.

"No. Not that we've picked up Captain. The American and Russians seemed to have joined forces in keeping an eye on the Yapikus ship in Iceland. They've been trying to interpret sounds coming from it, thinking that the inhabitants are trying to communicate with them".

"Sarah, is there any evidence that the Yapikus know that we're here?"

Sarah thought for a while and then came and stood close to the Captain "Again it's a no! But, even if they did, they know we are no threat to them. They send out so many unmanned ships, they know that some will always get back with fur samples to keep the trade going".

Ridoros, seeing Sarah so close to his grandson, could take it no more. "Captain, I'm going back to the field. You know where I am, if you want me".

THIRTY

OFFICER GWENDOLINE STIRWELL-TWINE AND HUSBAND WINSTON

While the Viriddion visitors were busy that day searching out more injured lions and tigers in the Africa and Indian Safari Parks, Winston and Gwendoline Stirwell-Twine had been busy on the ski slopes looking for Snow and the children.

The ski slopes were busy with lots of children. Winston and Gwendoline did their best to keep away from them, through fear of being recognised as the reporter who photographed Santa being taken away by police and accused of robbing a bank.

However, even though Winston covered his face with a scarf whilst skiing, he slipped and as his scarf came off, straight away he was recognised by one of the children.

Regrettably for Winston, one child jumping on him shouting "He's the Reporter, the Santa Hater" soon turned to hundreds of children jumping on him. Well that's what it felt like to Winston.

Winston tried calling out for Gwendoline's help but Gwendoline could only stand hopelessly watching, leaving Winston to think quick or lose his life, so he thought.

"No, No I'm a …. private detective. I have never believed that Santa was guilty. No, that's why I've come back to find the real person who did the break in!"

"Don't believe him" and "He's lying" were comments, amongst others being expressed by the children, piling on top of Winston.

"It's true. The police are only keeping Santa in their cell for his own safety in case the real robber thinks Santa can identify them". Winston couldn't believe what he had just said. Now he was in trouble with the police and the newspaper would certainly not want another story from him if they thought their reporter made up stories!

One by one the children looked at each other, and with some confusion, they climbed off Winston and carried on skiing.

Gwendoline rushed over to Winston and threw her arms around him. "Oh Winston, is that true. Do you really believe that Santa is innocent?"

THIRTY-ONE

LIONS AND CUBS

Meanwhile, the Viriddion visitors were approaching the Kenya Safari Park in Africa where there had been a report of a pride of lions suffering with an unidentified infection.

Just as they had done back in India, Liam and Brandon descended very low as they flew over and around the Park, then Jimmy and George began to groan as before with abdominal pain and Beth requested Liam to hover so they could quickly get down on the ground.

The Viriddion visitors were becoming more and more aware that they were running out of time in which to save the affected lions. It had been about twenty-four hours since the lions would have been attacked by the Yapikus and their infected wounds would be making them very weak and vulnerable to other wild animal that could prey on them.

Beth, Luke, Tayla, Jimmy, George and Snow, opened their doors and placed their feet into the stirrups at the end of the ropes that swung from their doors. The ropes descended to the ground within seconds.

They followed the twins to an area of dense shrubbery and looked around for any sign of the infected lions. Beth pointed over to a tree close by with long grass surrounding it. A lion's head could just about be seen.

Because of the long grass, they could not see how many lions were involved but they couldn't let that stop them from their task. So once again, whilst Luke and Beth prepared the equipment and medication Tayla and Snow began thinking of their mothers and singing. After a while, Beth joined in and in desperation Luke too.

It was obvious from the groans from the lions and the twins too that the lions were too sick to come to them.

"Luke, we have to go to them".

It was at that point that Liam and Brandon, who were hovering over the spot where the children were, saw a land rover approaching with some armed gamekeepers on board.

"Now, what are we going to do Liam? They'll take the children captive"

Liam pulled the ropes up, closed the doors and took the helicopter off across the park away from where the children were and hovered over a group of elephants.

"Hopefully, they will follow us for a while and not see the children until they finish what they need to do. I'll concentrate on the land rover, you concentrate on the children", urged Liam pushing the binoculars to Brandon.

Meanwhile, Beth and Luke had decided to creep up closer to the lions with Tayla and Snow but to leave the twins behind, who, at this stage, were in no fit state to creep or crawl anywhere.

As the four approached the long grass they could see four grown lions and three young ones. All of them had badly torn fur except the young ones. They were not dead but they were clearly very weak.

Beth immediately encouraged Tayla and Snow to carry on singing while Luke took a blood sample from the nearest lion and Beth injected the medication. Tayla spoke quietly to the lion as she stroked the thick fur around its neck. He was obviously the large male of the group and within a few minutes he began to try and get to his feet but kept falling back to the ground.

"It will take a little longer girls because they are much weaker. Oh, no ..." Beth could see a group of hyenas crouching in the grass, just a short way off. "Luke, they'll attack the lion cubs if they don't respond quickly enough".

Without discussing things further, Luke lifted up a cub and passed it to Tayla and another to Snow and another for himself and they made their way back to the tree where Jimmy and George were. "When the lions see the cubs missing, hopefully it might encourage them to get back on their feet quicker."

Jimmy and George were still crouched over in pain and, although they needed to be leaving, the helicopter was nowhere to be seen.

They could hear the occasional roar of the lions in the grass which implied to Beth that they were getting stronger and also making it clear to the hyenas that they were getting better but she was concerned about what to do with the cubs.

Just then they heard the helicopter arriving back and hovering over them. The ropes came down to them. The twins, with their pains slowly subsiding, began to make their way to the ropes, while the girls and Luke put the cubs down on the ground hoping they would run back to their family.

Suddenly the twins fell to the ground calling out in pain whilst holding their right legs. Beth knew that one of the cubs must have a damaged or broken right hind leg and when they checked, they soon realised which one it was.

Luke, again, instantly lifted up the cub that couldn't walk and brought it back to the tree where the boys were.

"Girls, get on the ropes", directed Beth as she saw the hyenas repositioning themselves in the long grassy area behind the tree where the twins were still groaning and holding their right legs. "Climb the tree twins. Luke help them".

The twins had not seen the hyenas and nor had Luke but, he had every faith in Beth's orders, especially if given in the urgent and authoritative manner in which she had just given it.

With George now up the tree, Beth quickly passed the lion cub to Jimmy as he was being given a leg up by Luke and shouted at them to get as high in the tree as possible, whilst they took a look at the cub's hind leg. She shouted that they would be back as soon as possible.

The moment Beth and Luke hit the ropes, the helicopter moved off across to the other side of the Park again, just in time to turn the oncoming land rover around again from the direction of the tree the twins were in.

While the land rover, with some angry men in it shouting and pointing guns at them, continued to follow the helicopter, Jimmy and George were looking at the lion cub's leg up in the tree.

"George, I thought it might be broken from the pain I've got but I think it's just been dislocated at the ankle. It has probably been trodden on"

"It doesn't look recent either. It looks as if the poor guys been hurting for a while. His Mum's probably been carrying him around up until now but, if we leave him as he is, as he gets bigger he will start lagging behind and he will soon be taken by that lot", indicating to the group of hyenas in the nearby grass. They were now making themselves very much known to the twins.

Jimmy and George manipulated the tiny bones in the little cub's ankle and as the pain went away in their own legs so the cub fell asleep in Jimmy's arms.

"That's no good, little man. We've got to get you back with your family".

Jimmy and George were trying to work out what to do. The helicopter was nowhere in sight, so it wasn't that difficult to decide to stay put and stay very, very still because the hyenas had now come to the tree trunk and were trying to jump up it.

"Hey guys, give us a break. George you try and talk to them, I'm whacked out. I'm more likely to cause them to attack us".

"I feel the same Jimmy. It's taking all my strength to hold on to this branch. Oh dear, don't look now but the lions are getting to their feet...the daddy is looking a little angry and we've got his son. Ok, what do we do now?"

Fortunately again, the twins didn't have to decide. They just had to sit and watch as the lions, after confronting the hyenas with some loud roaring, sent them off yelping with their tails between their legs.

Then, one of the lionesses came to the tree and stretched up to the two boys. The cub began to wake up and Jimmy reached down and slowly lowered the cub into the lioness's mouth. She lowered herself and the cub to the ground, with the rest of the family looking on, placed the cub on the ground and licked it all over before it ran off to join the other two cubs.

As the lions slowly walked away, the twins could see that the helicopter was back and two ropes were being lowered down into the tree. The twins didn't hesitate. They put their feet into the stirrups and the helicopter slowly raised the boys up out of the tree.

As the helicopter sped off across the park, the Viriddion children rested back, speechless and exhausted.

THIRTY-TWO

CAPTAIN GENESIS

Captain Genesis and the crew from the Animal Communication and Inter-Actionism Unit were also very tired and exhausted, even though they had only been watching the children on the earth monitor.

When Captain Genesis had seen what was going on in the Safari Parks he had asked Beth's deputy from the Unit to join him on the bridge. Julie was his and Beth's younger sister. She was two years younger than Beth but had the smile and long thick dark brown hair, similar to his and her older sister's.

"Julie, remind me why do the girls make that humming sound? I'm sure I'm meant to know that already but my mind at the moment seems to be busy with other things".

"Well, they don't have to make a sound but Snow and Tayla are still very young and full maturity of the

Viriddion communication skill takes years to develop. They are trying to find the communication level of the animal they are trying to interact with.

You know that Viriddions' believe animals have their own languages and the girls are trying to tune in, to be able to communicate with them. It is not necessarily the level of sound we hear that helps interact with the animals. The Viriddion theory is that, the tone of our sounds or vibrations caused, can appear friendly or aggressive".

"This sounds complicated", sighed Captain Genesis as he found a chair to sit on.

"No not really. The Earth people already recognise the fact that they can instruct particular animals with a whistle which is inaudible to the human ear!"

"Oh I see, so what your saying is that, the silent air or complete sound range that is expelled from the girls as they hum or sing will cause the animal to respond to them."

"Well it's not quite that simple Captain but, yes".

"So why can't they just use a whistle, or a pipe or something?"

"Because every animal is different and, just as you have taken years to train to do your job, the children and their families before them have taken years of training to expel the right silent pitch of air and sound that the animal they are trying to communicate with, will recognise. And: because the children are so young, Beth would be encouraging them to think of their mothers, which might broaden their breathing patterns".

"Thanks, Julie. Are you managing the families all right?" butted in Captain Genesis, quickly trying to change the subject as he felt the response was getting a little tense and personal.

"Yes thank you. Well, of course, I'm missing Beth but Old Ridoros pops in occasionally. He doesn't stay long; seems to get out of breath easily these days".

"Hmm, I suppose one hundred and twenty years old gives him an excuse to take it easy!"

As the Captain smiled at that thought, he turned in his chair and caught sight of Sarah from the Intelligence Unit in the monitor.

"Captain, we thought you might like to know the latest"

Sarah informed the Captain that negotiations had been going on between the Americans and Russians. It appeared that they had changed their minds and decided not to let the world have instant coverage about what they are doing with the UFO discovered on the ice in Iceland. Just in case it all went wrong, they only intended to feed certain information to the public.

Sarah went on to explain that a game keeper in Africa had reported a strange looking black helicopter hovering over their Park. The Game Keeper had managed to take a photo of the helicopter as it hovered over a herd of elephants and the aviation department had identified its registration number as being Scottish.

The description seemed to match the helicopter the police officers were looking for in Lapland and so they have let them know that the helicopter has now been genuinely identified.

"I wonder if Officer Stirwell-Twine is aware of this!"

THIRTY-THREE

OFFICER GWENDOLINE STIRWELL-TWINE AND HUSBAND WINSTON -V- INSPECTOR MOODY

Actually, Gwendoline was exceptionally happy. The strange helicopter was no longer a UFO. A real UFO in Iceland had been surrounded and, no doubt, appropriately dealt with and, best of all, her husband was no longer the baddie newspaper reporter but an important private detective that the children now loved.

Inspector Moody was not exactly happy that Winston had told the children that the police station was only keeping Santa in a safe place until they caught the real robbers of the bank because that wasn't really true.

On the other hand, the children were not so angry towards him and his officers and, in fact, the children now kept bringing in the occasional gift of an apple or a piece of chocolate for him or his officers, as a way of thanking them for keeping Santa safe.

Mind you, Inspector Moody and his officers had not exactly been doing nothing. He had ordered his officers to do a round the clock watch on the two elf workers called Alfred Pike and Ernest Pratt, following the interview Santa had with his lawyers.

Inspector Moody was not convinced that the two elf workers had anything to do with the bank robbery but, he wasn't going to frighten them away. He had to consider that they could either be working with Santa and that Santa had hidden the money and the three of them would leave together when he was free. Or: the elves did it alone and have hidden the money until Santa is placed in prison. But, if it was the latter, "why were the elves still hanging around the village. If that was the case, they would be long gone", he thought.

Inspector Moody and another officer had even very carefully searched the cottage the elves were staying in, when they were at work. They had been very careful to leave the place as they found it, not to raise the elves suspicions but they found absolutely nothing, only a very messy, smelly and untidy cottage which they were very pleased to leave in a hurry.

THIRTY-FOUR

RETURNING YAPIKUS PODS

Liam and Brandon were longing to sit back and rest a while, as they had travelled around and around the African Safari Park hovering over different groups of wildlife hoping to make the gamekeepers think that they may be newspaper reporters trying to get pictures.

Whilst chatting together, in the hope of keeping each other awake they approached a desert area, and saw a clearing in which they could put the helicopter down to have a rest, just for a short while, before aiming for Lapland again.

The helicopter came to a stop and the Viriddion visitors couldn't get out quick enough. The children were desperate to go the toilet and Liam and Brandon just wanted to lie down under the helicopter and rest in the shade for just half-an-hour.

The clearing had hills and caves and the odd raised rocky areas around it, so it wasn't difficult for Beth and Luke to find private areas for the children to do what they needed to do. The sun was going down and the air was cooling. Beth, Luke and the children made the most of having something to eat and drink, while Liam and Brandon rested.

After about hour longer than they had anticipated, Liam and Brandon got up and decided that they needed to stretch their legs. They strode up one of the hills a little further than the children had gone and as they were nearing the top of the hill they thought they would just go a little further to see what was on the other side.

The sky was dark now with just a few stars dotted about but, it didn't stop Liam and Brandon seeing an object resting in the clearing on the other side of the hill, an object that they would rather not have seen.

Liam brought out the night binoculars and took a look. He then handed them to Brandon, who then beckoned Beth, Luke and the children to join them. The Viriddion visitors, one by one, looked silently through the binoculars and had, no doubt, that they were looking at a Yapikus spaceship.

Liam took the binoculars back and looked around the area. There was no one to be seen.

"What are we going to do?" urged Jimmy.

"Blow them up!" quickly replied Jimmy and George.

"Good thinking boys and I would be very tempted too, if we carried explosives", laughed Liam.

"Liam, why are they still there. Have they just arrived?" asked Luke.

"I think we will know sooner or later. If they have just arrived, they will open their portals and send out groups of small mechanical pods. On the other hand, if they've been here a while, they'll be opening their portals to let the pods return. The pods only seem to travel, backwards and forwards, when the sun has gone down".

"Everyone quick, follow me. Snow you stay put. Everyone else do exactly as I tell you" ordered Liam.

Liam ran to the shining oval metal object and pulled himself up on to the ridge of the ship. He helped all of the others up to a platform that ran around the ship just under the closed portals.

Snow, froze on the spot, she had no idea what Liam had planned. She could only trust him not to get anyone of them hurt.

"There are four portals" instructed Liam. "You must keep low because the portals will open outwards and downwards. As soon as they begin to open, you will need to put pressure on the portal to stop it from opening. Beth and Tayla you concentrate on that one, Luke that one, Brandon that one and I'll take this one. They will begin to open simultaneously so when I shout push, you must all push hard on the portals".

It was just then that Snow noticed, what looked like a flock of birds approaching and shouted "Flock of birds incoming".

Liam shouted "Push. Push. Don't let the portals open. Keep pushing until I say jump and then drop under the rim of the ship".

The group of small objects continued to approach the ship and when only seconds away Liam shouted "Jump.

Jump" and they all jumped off and found shelter under the rim of the ship, while the metal pods bombarded the closed portals and then fell to the ground.

"Run. Run" shouted Liam.

The Viriddions' did not hesitate. They knew they needed to get out of there and back over to the other side of the hill where Snow was watching.

No sooner had they reached Snow, there was huge explosion behind them and they looked back to a black hole in the ground.

The Viriddion visitors silently made their way back to the helicopter, climbed back on board and sped back to the Lapland village, wondering how they were going to report what had just happened.

THIRTY-FIVE

CAPTAIN GENESIS

Reporting back, however, was not really an issue on this occasion because Roger and Sarah from the Intelligence Unit had picked up the Viriddions' encounter with the Yapikus on the viewer. For a long while, the crew sat in silence but then the student pilots had become very angry.

"Captain, you've got to let us take the transporters out. Liam and Brandon need help", demanded Mikey.

"Oh, I understand where you're coming from but neither you nor your transporters are registered on Earth. There's nothing that you can do. You would be picked up immediately. Actually, thinking about it, there is something you can do Mikey, just make sure those transporters are ready to go just in case and you and your colleagues piloting skills are A1 ....

If the worst comes to the worst, we might have to take the risk but, until then, just make sure you and the transporters are ready".

THIRTY-SIX

DAVID SEYMOUR

Meanwhile, David Seymour was reflecting over the past few years that had led him to be a Santa in Lapland. He had returned to Earth, just five years ago to be an E-Contact, just after his Viriddion wife had died. Such a decision was not unusual. The reason he left Earth as a young twenty-five year old qualified Veterinarian, was to learn more about communication and interaction skills at the Viridis University.

He hadn't intended to stay so long with the Viriddions'. However, like many other young earthlings who visited the Planet Viridis for various training purposes, they experienced the plight of the dying planet and the Viriddion race. Many fell in love with a Viriddion, staying on one of their underground ships longer than they had planned.

David Seymour's thoughts were interrupted. He

thought he heard that little girl, called Snow. Since he had been kept at the police station he was always hearing the children calling out to him and, occasionally a police officer would play the Santa role and let them ask him for a particular present for Christmas.

What he didn't want was to see Snow. Snow was in great danger, if she was a Viriddion. She must not be seen to be connected to him at all. In fact, if Viridis 6000 had arrived, all of the crew were in danger but, he didn't know who to trust any more.

He was, in one sense desperate to leave the police station and pleased that his Viriddion help sign had been recognised by the young men who visited claiming to be his lawyers but, on the other hand, he knew that a Yapikus trader might recognise the sign too.

"It's all right Santa, we'll have you out for Christmas. There is a private detective on your case now. He'll get you out", reassured Inspector Moody, who happened to be passing and noticed Santa's downcast look.

"Oh, by the way, Mrs Moody told me to let you know that Heidi's pups are doing well and are in the process of being re-homed. She only has two males left"

"I expect Bertie is one of them", smiled David.

"Yes, he is but, I think he's the best natured and cleverest. They only reject him because we tell them he had a poorly time when he was first born, being the last and all that. It doesn't help when he pretends to be asleep when interested buyers visit. We know he is only pretending because as soon as the visitors go, he jumps up and starts licking the dog that been chosen as if he's pleased they've been chosen and not him".

"Maybe he thinks if he's not chosen he can stay with his Mum".

"Well we thought that, but the strange thing is, Heidi pushes him away if he gets too close to her - so Mrs Moody is absolutely adamant that Bertie's not staying".

"Well then, he's obviously waiting for a very special buyer" reassured David.

David Seymour rested back on his bed, after all he had nothing better to do at present. However, talking about Bertie, had caused him to reflect back to when he held little Bertie in his hands.

He was only a few days old and very limp. Mrs Moody had taken Bertie, the Siberian Husky pup to the village Vet who had said that he had obviously received neurological damage during birth and there wasn't anything they could do for him.

David Seymour had met Mrs Moody leaving the Vet surgery very upset about the decision and he had offered to try and help Bertie.

It wasn't unusual for David Seymour to be asked for last minute advice from the occasional owner with a sick animal, especially since the villagers learnt that he was a retired Veterinary Surgeon.

However, Bertie was a little different because he was so young and he hadn't wanted to take him away from his mother's milk, so he visited the pup four times a day to massage and talk to it.

He bathed Bertie in special oils every day whilst talking to him and after two weeks he was as strong as his siblings. Heidi always greeted her pup with lots of licking after each session, demonstrating the bond between them was still there.

He couldn't understand therefore why Heidi should now be pushing him away unless she was trying to prepare herself for the time she would have to let him go.

OFFICER GWENDOLINE STIRWELL-TWINE AND HUSBAND WINSTON

Winston Stirwell was definitely a changed man, according to his wife. Gwendoline had caught sight of Beth, Luke and the children in the village the next morning and she had beckoned them into a café, so that she could tell them about her husband, the new detective for Santa.

Gwendoline had continued to explain that her husband had been called up on another story for a few days, which she thought was to do with sick animals. However, he would return for Santa again, very soon.

"That's great", said Snow, whilst sucking on the straw of her milkshake "He must be free for Christmas Day".

"And so he will. Now tell me about your day yesterday Snow? Did you enjoy it?"

"Yes, we saw lions and tigers and lots of other animals and the Yapikus".

"Cor, I wish I could have been with you, I don't think I've seen a Yapikus, what does it look like?"

Beth, Luke, Tayla, Jimmy and George all looked at each other in astonishment and opened their mouths to volunteer an answer of sorts but, as usual Snow answered "It was like an enormous sleeping tortoise"

"Oh not very cuddly then. I prefer animals with lovely soft fur".

And, before Snow could answer that, Beth said that they must be excused, saying that, even though the children were on holiday, they still had lots of writing to do.

"Oh you poor things; see you later" she called out as she watched the children and their teachers walk off down through the village towards their log cabin.

Gwendoline was not the only one watching them, and she knew it. Winston had made some enquiries at the police station about any visitors that Santa had received since being accused of robbing the village bank and he had been told that the drivers for the children from the orphanage were acting as Santa's lawyers.

Winston was not away as she had just told the children but, he had the drivers under surveillance. She hated lying to the children but, she thought, that if their drivers were criminals they ought not to be involved with the children.

Of course, Inspector Moody had made it clear to Winston that they had no reason to suspect the children or their drivers were involved in the robbery but couldn't really stop Winston from carrying out his own investigations.

THIRTY-EIGHT

TWINS VISIT TO POLICE STATION

The children spent the rest of that day in their log cabin. They were all very tired and, in any event, Liam and Brandon needed to spend a short time for maintenance on the carrier and then call into the village police station to see Inspector Moody.

"Can George and I come with you, Liam? We won't get in your way".

"Come on then you two and woe betides you if you do", laughed Liam.

It was unusual to see Liam laughing. It wasn't that he wasn't happy with his job, as he loved piloting any kind of craft – aeroplane, auto-mobile or boat. But there was the pressure of the recent loss of his Viriddion parents and the important role of being responsible for transporting the children around on Earth together with the added responsibility of trying to keep his younger brother Brandon safe beside him. He was beginning to experience and sense the real dangers that they were in while visiting the Planet Earth.

The visit to see Inspector Moody was not one that they particularly wanted at present because he was still awaiting Rubin McDonald in Scotland to get back to him about a few queries he had.

However, when they arrived back from Kenya they found a note slipped under the cabin door addressed to Liam Logan.

It had been hand written requesting him to call into the station as soon as possible and signed by Inspector Moody.

The Logan brothers had rather hoped that, this was good news regarding Santa but, they didn't want to raise the children's hopes too soon and, decided to treat the visit very casually.

When the four of them arrived at the police station, Inspector Moody greeted them as if they were old friends.

"Oh, thanks for coming Mr Logan. No problem. No problem. I'm just trying to tie up a few loose ends. A couple of my officer's interviewed the children, a few days ago, who said that you were their drivers. So I was just wondering, why did you say you were Santa's lawyer?"

Just as the Inspector asked that question, Liam caught sight of Jimmy and George sitting either side of him, and he and Brandon couldn't stop themselves from laughing.

Jimmy and George had seen the officers' hats on the side cabinet and placed them on their heads, pulled up chairs either side of the Inspector, on the opposite side of the desk to the Logan brothers and were copying the Inspector's serious face expressions and arm movements.

"Boys behave. I'm sorry Inspector", said Liam, nudging Brandon, trying to get him to maintain a serious composure while trying to decide how he was going to answer the question.

He thought he heard his Mother's saying: "Just tell the truth, Son". But, he thought it was probably because, over the years she had said that to him on many occasions.

"As you know", started Liam "The children are orphans and we had heard that Snow's grandfather was possibly working as Santa in Lapland. When we arrived, he had been arrested and, as his lawyers are based in Scotland, we were acting for Santa's lawyers, when we visited him".

"Who is Snow?"

"The youngest of the children; the one with wavy blond hair" said Liam.

"Oh yes, the officers' told me about the little one, that always carries a big bag around with her. But, why didn't she mention at the time the officers' interviewed her, that she was Santa's Granddaughter".

"That's because she doesn't know", replied the brothers together.

"You see, we didn't want to give her false information, until we had checked it out. As far as Snow is concerned, we came to Lapland to visit Santa and visit a zoo, as she loves animals".

"Whilst we're talking about Santa", continued Liam "Have you any more information that could help us put a case together for him … …"

Inspector Moody let them know that the newspaper reporter, Winston Stirwell, had pledged his services to be Santa's private detective and he promised to keep them informed about any new information.

When the Logan brothers and twins left, Inspector Moody sat down with a cup of tea and biscuits brought in by one of the officers' who had interviewed the children earlier and who had been listening in on the visit today from another office.

"Well, what do you think officer? Do you think Santa and the orphan children are working together in this case?"

THIRTY-NINE

WINSTON STIRWELL THE DETECTIVE

Well, whatever the officer thought was immaterial, as far as Winston Stirwell was concerned. He was convinced that the children's drivers were hiding something and, when he saw them leave the police station with the twins, he was even more convinced that they were in league with Santa and had used the twins to get in and see Santa.

Winston had just picked up his wife's favourite love story video and a box of chocolates because he had promised her a special cosy night in - but this was far too important to miss.

It was late afternoon but still quite light. He kept his distance as he followed the young men and boys to the ski slopes where they rented two jet skis. As Liam and Jimmy

150

on one and Brandon and George on the other sped off, Winston had to move quickly to rent a jet ski for himself or he would lose sight of them.

As Winston rounded a corner, he was just able to see the two jet skis in front of him, disappear around another corner, and as he reached that corner they turned yet another until they arrived and stopped outside the village bank. Winston, when he saw them stop, stopped and remained hidden, while he watched them go around to the back of the bank.

Winston at this point, was getting excited. He felt like a real detective. There were other people walking through the village and occasionally on a jet ski, so he knew he didn't look that odd.

"Well maybe a little odd", he thought to himself as he noticed his colourful hand knitted scarf that Gwendoline had knitted for him years ago. He loved it but thought it best to try and hide it further under his jacket because he didn't want to draw attention to himself.

Winston slowly followed the Logan brothers' around to the back of the bank and continued following them as they drove off, up through an avenue of trees until they reached Santa's grotto, where he observed them get off their skis.

Parking further back amongst the trees he watched the young men and twin boys walk around the grotto as if they were looking for something. "Ah", thought Winston "Santa must have told them where to find the stolen cash".

In one sense Winston was right, the Logan brothers and the twins were looking for something. Inspector Moody had made them aware of the evidence they had found on the night of the break in of the village bank, and the particular route the person on a jet ski took from the back of the village bank to a small back door to Santa's grotto. And, they were hoping to find some new evidence to offer Inspector Moody.

The Logan brothers told the twins to remain outside and keep an eye on the jet skis whilst they went into the grotto. They explained to the head elf at the reception area, who they were and that they would just like to look over the grotto.

The elf along with the other helpers and even the temporary Santa were extremely pleased to meet them, saying that they didn't believe that David Seymour broke into the bank because he was a really nice man.

They noted that the little door at the rear of the grotto opened into the stock area where other elves were wrapping presents. They asked whether all the elves were on duty but were told that two elves called Ernest and Alfred were off duty for the next few days.

The Logan brothers thanked Santa and his elves for their help and went back out to the twins, who were, as usual making the most of the snow as missiles.

"Liam, I think we're being watched from back there amongst the trees", George said, throwing a snow missile at Liam trying not to let it look obvious to the onlooker that he had been spotted.

"We think it's our friend Winston Stirwell" laughed Jimmy. "He's the only person we know with such a pretty scarf".

"Hmm, he's obviously playing at being a detective. Come on, let's drop off these skis and get back to the cabin".

FORTY

ERNIE AND ALFIE

Ernest Pike and Alfred Pratt had spent their day off, hovering around outside the Viriddion visitor's log cabin, in the hope that they would be going out for the day and they could try again to retrieve the present, which they still thought was in Snow's bag.

It had got to the end of the day and they had decided to start walking back to their cottage. Well, not their cottage because they knew full well, it really belonged to Santa.

Just as they stood up from the log they had been sitting on close to the cabin, Ernest noticed Liam, Brandon, Jimmy and George walking down from the village towards to them.

"Alfie, quick cross over to the other side of the lane and look on the ground as you walk. We don't want them to recognise us?"

"Hi, Ernie and Alfie", Jimmy called across to them. "See you on the slopes again soon", joined in George.

"Er, good disguise, Ernie!"

Back in the cabin the twins informed the others about their day whilst Liam and Brandon spent time on their transporter in the garage.

"Don't you think it strange, Liam, why that chap Winston should be following us?"

"No, not really but, I'm more concerned as to why those two elves should be hanging around our cabin on their day off. I think if we don't hear back from Rubin soon, we'll have to pay him a visit".

FORTY-ONE

CAPTAIN GENESIS

Back in the field on Viridis 6000, Old Ridoros was resting on his lounger. He had felt the need to rest back with his Visionars. In fact, since landing on Earth again, he had felt the need for the comfort of his Visionars most days.

He found himself reflecting on the day he found himself on the Viridis 6000 for the first time......

..... The weather was bad, murky, misty and over cast. He was ready for this Charge. His sword was raised in readiness in expectation of the slashing and slicing. He could hear the other solders on their horses bounding in front of him and on either side of him. Yes, he was ready for this fight for his country, his life, like all the troops alongside him but: as a cavalry man he was not only fighting for his life, he was fighting for the life of his horse Ridoros.

Ridoros was his best friend. He had groomed, fed and slept alongside him, in readiness for this Charge ..... It had been expected for days.... Then he saw and felt, what he didn't really want to experience again, the horses falling around him, the screams and shouts from all about him.

Among the screams and shouts he too was shouting, falling ... . He was falling because Ridoros was falling. He could hear slashing of swords and the noise from the infantry behind him but something was wrong, very wrong about this advance.

... ... He could hear the enemy who were advancing on them, now slowly retreating and he remembered thinking "the advance must have been a success". He couldn't see properly and apart from the pain all around his neck the pain in his right eye was severe. As the smoke and mist began to clear he could just about see why he and his best friend Ridoros could not move ... ... The cavalry had been led straight into a valley coiled high with barbed wire. The barbed wire was cutting deep into Ridoros's flesh and he was clearly in pain. ... ... He saw himself struggling to get to his feet to stop the wire from cutting deeper into Ridoros, but as he moved, the pain from the barbed wire hooked around his own neck and was holding him fast making him useless to his friend. ... ... He saw himself shout out to his friend "Ridoros. Ridoros" and then remembering no more......".

Old Ridoros sat up from his lounger. How could he forget his last Charge with the 4th Dragoons at the battle of Mons. Nor the first memories he had when he woke up in a hospital with bandages over and around his head and neck and being told by a nurse that he had lost an eye and would probably have deep scaring around his neck and then sadly that they had not been able to save his horse.

He had asked the nurse why she called him Mr Ridoros because, although he wasn't sure, he didn't think that was his name. She said that every time he came to and she kept asking him what his name was, he would call out the name "Ridoros".

When he was well and able to walk about the hospital, he soon learned that he was no longer on Earth but on a spaceship called Viridis 6000 being called Ridoros.

Over time, he learnt about Viriddions' on their Planet and attended the Viridis's College via the Visionars and studied Terrestrial Threats to Animal Life.

Oh yes, he did consider returning to Earth next time the Viriddions visited but, he fell in love with the beautiful Lithusania and then, it didn't matter where he lived.

"I could have been on the Moon", he thought smiling to himself.

"Granddad, there you are", Captain Genesis sat down beside Old Ridoros. He noticed the Visionars beside him and knew that he been reflecting over his life. "I'm sorry Granddad, you were obviously deep in thought and I have just disturbed you. I sometimes forget that you must be missing your Son, my Father".

"I've lived far too long Genesis. All I seem to do is sleep and dream. I don't know how I can help you!"

"Well, you are the only person left on the ship with a deep understanding about the Yapikus. I need you to take a look at the recording we have on the children in Africa and the ship that's landed in Iceland, I need to know why it's still there. You can then lay back on your lounger and set the Visionar on 111", smiled Captain Genesis as he walked off.

"Oh, very funny, that's a sleep zone!"

FORTY-TWO

WINSTON STIRWELL

When Winston returned that evening, it was much later than his wife had anticipated and Gwendoline was not exactly happy because the special supper she had prepared for her husband was spoiled.

However, after he explained the importance of being a private detective; and the need for a special wife who would understand his coming and going at all hours, he produced the box of chocolates, and all was forgiven.

After eating the chocolates whilst watching her favourite film, Gwendoline climbed into bed to tell her husband about the latest information from her UFO Office in the USA.

"They say that they have got a special team, trying to decode the sounds that are coming from the ship. ... ... Apparently, it's just been sitting there. ... ... The Army are suggesting that it should be blown up, to demonstrate to other aliens that they can't just visit our Planet without clearing their landing first. ... ... The President is saying that he wants to be seen shaking the hands of the aliens. ... ... They've put a no access area around the ship and no fly zone over it to prevent the media and public knowing about it. ... ... I had to swear that I wouldn't let you know about the ship ..... Oh dear", Gwendoline suddenly realised that she was talking to her husband and looked over to him, just as she heard him snore. "Thank goodness for that, you're asleep and you haven't heard a word I've said".

Winston of course, wasn't really asleep. He was a freelance reporter. He missed nothing. He had acquired a skill for retrieving information he wasn't meant to know about: Information which he didn't need to decipher or moralize on. All he needed to do was just to write it down for other people to do that.

But: he had a problem, since taking on the role of a detective. Winston found himself trying to work out why certain people were doing certain things, in contrast to his usual role of simply taking a photo and writing a statement like "Lawyers for Santa – desperately seek evidence to free him".

The problem was that Winston had not thought about other people's feelings before. An issue that had not concerned him before now or, at least, before he married Gwendoline.

FORTY-THREE

VISIT TO ZOO AND SEA LION

This morning was the morning the Viriddion visitors were determined to get to the Zoo. They had some final data they had to get from certain animals before they returned to the Viridis 6000.

"Are we definitely going back to the ship Beth in the next couple of days?" enquired Snow, as she ate her breakfast, not forgetting to share a little with Lemmie who kept poking his head out of her bag.

"It's a difficult decision Snow. It would be nice to find a house on Earth and settle here, especially now as a number of the children have lost their Viriddion parents. But, if the Yapikus are going to be regular visitors to Earth, we can't fight them on our own. We might need Old Ridoros's help!"

It was not long after that, that the Viriddion visitors were on their way in their black people carrier.

And: yes, and you can probably guess, the off duty elves Ernest and Alfred were not far behind them. They had overheard the Logan brothers telling the shop assistant that they were off to the Zoo today, as they bought the daily paper.

However, Ernst had an idea about dressing up smartly in some of David Seymour's unused clothes, so that the children wouldn't recognise them.

"After all", chuckled Ernest "Santa won't need them in prison", as he finished dressing in, tartan trousers and brown casual jacket with a trilby hat.

"Ernie, you're so clever, they'll never recognise us like this. And, the children will just think you're my Dad taking me to the zoo, dressed like this".

They came out of David Seymour's bedroom and admired themselves in the long mirror in the hallway, which reflected a very large Ernie and a very small Alfie alongside him.

"I presume these school clothes belonged to one of his children", suggested Alfie as he looked at a picture on the wall of a young David Seymour, a beautiful silver blonde haired lady and two small children, in their school uniforms. "I wonder why they never visit him?"

Once the Viriddion visitors reached the Zoo, Liam and Brandon decided not to go in with the children because they had maintenance to carry out on the carrier and some phone calls to make.

Tayla, Jimmy, George and Snow could not get in

through the entrance gates quickly enough. Even though they had recently seen some tigers and lions, the time with them was fleeting and because they were sick they were difficult to communicate with.

They had so looked forward to visiting Earth. Animals had been quite extinct from the surface of Viridis for thousands of years now. So the children had only seen the large animals, such as the lion, tiger, polar bear and so on, via pictures or films on their Visionars and from tales their parents would have passed on to them.

"Sea lions", shouted Snow as she ran over to the Sea Lion house, followed by the other children. The walls in the house were made of glass and the sea lions kept sliding into the water and diving down through to ground level, as if saying hello to the children and then swimming back up to the surface excitedly.

The children made their way to the sea lions' outside pool, where they were about to be fed by the keeper.

Whilst the children were busy with the sea lions, a smartly dressed man wearing a trilby hat and accompanied by a young boy, joined the children. The children didn't take too much notice because there were lots of parents and children looking at the sea lions with them but, every now and then, Snow caught the boy looking at her bag rather than the sea lions.

"Tayla, that boy keeps looking at me, do you think he knows us?" whispered Snow trying not to let the boy hear. He was standing rather close to her.

"No I don't think so", whispered back Tayla as she clapped her hands and jumped up and down with excitement at the sea lions as they came forward one by one to the keeper for a fish.

Snow wanted so much to watch the sea lions being fed but because the boy kept looking at her she thought it might be rude not to say hello, in case they did know him, so she moved over and crept in between the twins and whispered ....

"Jimmy and George, do we know this boy behind me because he looks familiar?"

The twins looked a little annoyed that they would have to stop watching the sea lions but, they turned around, looked in all directions and then whispered "No".

Snow wasn't that convinced but because she didn't like the idea of the boy standing so close to her bag, she moved up to the end of the railings so that her bag was safe between a wall and herself, whilst getting as close to the sea lions as she could.

The sea lions intermittently took the fish and slid into the pool before popping out of the water again, clapping their flippers together, and making barking sounds whilst balancing balls on their noses.

Snow couldn't stop clapping and the sea lions kept swimming quite close to her. The boy found his way back beside her and again Snow found herself getting a little worried. Just at that time, a sea lion popped his head out of the water, looked at Snow and then the boy standing beside, ran a flipper over the top of the water and sprayed the boy.

All the children looking on were clapping and laughing. The boy didn't think it was that funny and moved back to his Dad to get dried off and Snow waved to the sea lion and said "Thanks, you're right; I must keep an eye on him".

With the feeding of the sea lions finished the Viriddion visitors moved on around the Zoo to the Tiger House. The twins knew they needed to get a foot print from the tiger and measurements from its tail. The data they would be collecting could be used to compare their well-being to their ancestors either held in captivity or free in the wild.

Of course, it was possible that they could have asked the keeper for this information but the children needed to know that the data was accurate and up to date and that they could also test their communication skills out, whilst obtaining the samples.

Looking into the cage, the children could see four very sleepy tigers. Two were up at tree height, with one hanging over a thick branch. Another was lying on a platform alongside the branch and two more were lying on the ground not far from each other.

"Hmm, at least they don't look hungry" smiled Beth at Luke.

"No, thank goodness", smiled Luke getting out Liam's binoculars from his pocket. "Don't you need these boys?"

"Oh, yes but, the tigers all seem to be hiding their tails, so this isn't going to be easy!"

George took the binoculars. The binoculars had a measuring feature, which provided the length and diameter of an object, once focused on it. Such a devise was just the thing they needed when it came to obtaining the measurement of a tiger's tail. But, only if they could get sight of the tails and get the tigers to keep them still long enough for a recording.

As the children tried desperately to get one tigers attention, Beth and Luke sat on a nearby seat and watched, as if they were the proud children's parents. They weren't exactly sitting close together, only because Luke considered that he should demonstrate a professional respect for Beth. Of course, he would love to have sat closer and he was wondering how he could, maybe, accidentally move up closer without it seeming obvious.

Over the past few days working so closely with Beth and sharing her responsibilities and worries over the children, Luke had become very fond of Beth and had begun to wonder how Beth felt about him. On that thought, he figured that, next time he encouraged the children, he will stand up and then sit down, only a little closer to Beth.

It was obvious how difficult it would be to get a tiger to do what you want it to do, especially when there's a high fence between you with keepers watching on. So when the children finally got one of the tigers to come and lay closer to the fence where the children were standing, Jimmy balanced on George's shoulders with the binoculars focused on the tiger's tail, and shouted "Got it. Got it", Beth and Luke spontaneously leapt to their feet with delight clapping and cheering.

"Oh hi children, what's the celebration", requested Gwendoline as she joined the Viriddion visitors.

She took off the colourful silk scarf from over her head and wrapped it around her neck, freeing up her freshly permed hair to the fresh air. "Winston suggested a drive and I thought it might be nice to visit the Zoo. You look as if you're enjoying yourself Snow".

"Yes", replied Snow politely, but still laughing from the sight of Jimmy nearly falling on top of Tayla. "Do you want to look at the tiger's tail?"

"Ooo, no thanks, another time maybe, I'll just sit here for a while and watch."

Gwendoline brushed her hand over the spare seat and sat down precariously between Beth and Luke.

"Winston not with you then?" asked Beth looking around and catching a glimpse of a now glum looking Luke.

"No. He decided when we got here that he had some important notes he needed to write up, so he suggested that I come in and enjoy myself".

FORTY-FOUR

CAPTAIN GENESIS

While the Viriddion visitors were at the Zoo, Captain Genesis and his crew were busy keeping an eye on the American and Russian ships, which were still encircling the Yapikus ship, trying to decide what they were going to do with it,

Old Ridoros had informed them that a ship of that size had no living person in it and that it was simply a ship controlled from a much larger ship or control base on another planet. He wanted to make it clear however, that the people controlling the manufacture of animal fur in this way, were constantly changing their tactics.

Old Ridoros had also informed them that a ship is normally programmed to land only for about four hours in one place. He therefore suggested that if the ship was still there it had either malfunctioned or it was a decoy, for a massive invasion normally miles away.

He continued to explain that if it had malfunctioned, it will be programmed to destroy itself. In any event, if a ship is tampered with by outside contact, they are normally programmed to explode.

Roger Baker from the Viridis 6000 Intelligence and Sarah his daughter were continually updating Captain Genesis with the conversation and intentions of the American UFO Department.

Sarah was again on the bridge reporting that Officer Gwendoline Stirwell-Twine had sent a message to the UFO department saying that her husband was now working as a private detective trying to solve the Lapland village bank robbery and that would give her the opportunity to spend more time with the children.

She had explained that the children whom she met in Scotland were now at the Lapland village and, although they were supposed to be orphans on holiday, she now believed they were the aliens from the space ship she had seen on their honeymoon.

Officer Gwendoline had continued to explain that she needed to remain in Lapland longer to observe the "supposed" orphan visitors.

"Well, that's not good news. I thought she would be a problem. Sarah, what did her boss think about that?" enquired Captain Genesis as he fiddled about on a monitor in front of him, trying hard not to look at this beautiful Sarah in front of him.

Again, Captain Genesis was finding it very difficult to

concentrate on his job, whenever Sarah was around, and so he tried desperately to avoid eye contact when discussing a situation that may be putting the children at risk.

"Her Chief appears to want her to return to the office and believes she's either lost the plot or so besotted with her new husband that she will make any excuse to spend more time with him.

On the other hand, our E-Contact in her office appears to be encouraging the Chief to allow her to pursue her suspicions. I'm not sure why he's doing that, though!" and as he looked up, Sarah gave a little smile and left the bridge.

"She smiled. Yes she did. She smiled at me!" Captain Genesis said to himself under his breath. He quickly tried to think of another question to hold her on the bridge, when Julie, his younger sister arrived to inform him that the Animal Unit had been observing the lions and tigers that the children had vaccinated and they all appeared well, which helped him to focus back on the real problem.

"Captain, I can't wait for the children to return. We'll be able to get the results of the blood samples they took. I presume the children will be back?"

FORTY-FIVE

SAMSON THE TIGER AND SNOWFLAKE

Meanwhile, as Beth, Luke and Gwendoline looked on, the children tried to decide how to get a foot print from the tiger that had come close to the fence where the children were standing. As usual, the young boy, who was paying a lot of attention to Snow was still her constant shadow and somewhat annoying to her and she was getting the feeling that he was familiar to her and this made her feel uneasy.

"Boys, how are we going to get the foot print from Samson", said Tayla trying to organize the situation.

"Samson?" joined in Snow, trying hard to get involved and free from the young boy following her "How do you know his name is Samson, Tayla?"

"The notice over there says that the friendly Siberian

tiger is called Samson and as he appears to be the friendly one, I reckon he must be Samson".

Snow ran off to read the notice, with the young boy in tow whilst the twins and Tayla continued to discuss the situation.

"George, how about, asking Samson to walk forward just a little further, so that he puts one of his paws in that little muddy puddle. We could then measure the print with the binoculars".

"Good idea Jimmy. You get ready with the binoculars because the print won't stay that long as the mud is too wet".

With the game plan in hand, Tayla and George went to work encouraging Samson to move forward to place a paw in the muddy puddle.

Hearing the excitement, Snow ran to the fence with the children and joined in with the plan calling: "Come on Samson, just one more step forward".

Samson looked at Snow, rubbed his head up and down on the fence, moved forward and slowly lifted up a paw and placed it in the puddle, retrieving it just as quickly.

"Ye ha, successful", exclaimed Jimmy.

"Thank you so much Samson", said Snow leaning forward and blowing him a kiss.

The boy, seeing Snow preoccupied, placed his hand in her bag. Samson, having taken his paw out of the muddy puddle, took one look at the boy, placed his paw back into the puddle and flicked some mud up through the fence and into the boy's face which stopped him immediately in his sneaky pursuit.

Alfie, the off duty elf, disguised as a school boy, gave a

yell and ran over to Ernest, the other off duty elf, disguised as his Father.

"Thanks Samson", whispered Snow walking over to Gwendoline.

"So what's so special about that tiger, Snow?"

There are only about 400 Siberian tigers left in the wild and about the same amount in captivity on Earth. It's very important that we look after the ones in captivity as well as those in the wild."

"Well, yes. And, where did you learn that?"

"From that notice board over there of course", replied Snow, echoing the matter of fact manner of Tayla earlier, as she ran back over to join Tayla and the twins. They were making their way to the next animal house, as aeroplanes.

Snow took Tayla's hand. She was so proud to have Tayla as a sister. Well, she knew Tayla wasn't her real sister. In fact, Snow didn't have any brothers or sisters. However, over these past couple of weeks, Snow had grown very fond of Tayla and often found herself thinking how clever she was.

After all, she was eight years older than her. Of course, Snow had grown just as fond of the twins but they always wanted to play at being aeroplanes or fight in pretend missile games, which could be quite annoying sometimes, especially when she just wanted to sit quietly and play with Lemmie.

Thinking of Lemmie, Snow placed her free hand into her bag and found a cold and shivery Lemmie.

"Tayla, Lemmie's not well" cried Snow as she brought Tayla to a stop.

Tayla placed her hand into the bag and felt Snow's little friend.

"He might just need another jumper in there with him. The sun is bright to day but the air is cold. Go and take Lemmie to Beth", suggested Tayla indicating to the three adults walking behind them a little way off.

Snow took her bag over to Beth and asked Beth if she could hold her bag a moment but, before she could whisper quietly to Beth the reason why, Gwendoline reached over and took the bag saying "Oh, let me Snow, I'd love to carry your bag".

Snow looked horrified but remained speechless. Beth thought it was strange that Snow should be giving up her bag and then noticed Tayla's horrified face.

"Oh, Snow, you could at least put Loppie in your pocket to lighten the load for poor old Gwendoline" jumped in Beth, quickly taking the bag and rummaging through it and finally taking out Loppie and passing him to Snow, who was still standing speechless, before handing the bag back to Gwendoline.

"Loppie! Who is Loppie?" enquired Gwendoline "Oh, is this your friend Snow?"

"Yes, my Mother made him for me, when I was first born".

"Hmm, I can see why you call him Loppie because he's got big floppy ears like a rabbit but I didn't know rabbits' have long tails!"

"My Mother was probably thinking about another type of rabbit to the one you know".

"Yes, I suppose so", replied Gwendoline stepping forward with Snow's bag over her shoulder.

Snow moved around between Beth and Luke. Beth took Snow's hand, saying "Here, warm your hand up in my pocket for a while" and as she placed it in Beth's pocket she felt a little Lemmie snuggled up in one of Beth's gloves and much warmer than he was earlier.

With a sigh of relief, Snow joined the rest of the children who were now gathering at the Polar Bears Sanctuary and leaning over the fence. She could see it was empty. "Oh, that's a shame", she thought.

As the children began to move on, Snow requested that they stop, saying that something was wrong.

"What's up Snow? What are you feeling?" queried George.

"I just feel sad, very sad. I feel like crying".

Tayla ran over to a side door. It had a high small window, too high for the children to see in; so George volunteered to give Jimmy a lift up to have a peep in. Jimmy explained that he could see a pure white young Polar Bear, walking about in and out of a small pool. It looked very lonely and sad, and was making a continuous whining sound.

"It's lonely, sad and crying. We need to get in to talk to it", cried Snow.

When Beth, Luke and Gwendoline caught up with the children they found all of them looking very upset. They decided to find a keeper who was very informative:

"Actually it's a very sad case … … we call her Snowflake … … she was brought to us early this morning as an emergency place of safety ... ... she was found alongside her Mother who had been attacked by something or someone and her wounds had become infected and had killed her ... ... it appears that Snowflake's Mother must have been protecting her little one from the person or animal that attacked her because Snowflake doesn't appear to have any injuries ... if she had been left to fend for herself she would have died. Being here, she stands a chance of survival even if it is not her natural environment."

Beth explained that Luke and her were teachers and were visiting the Zoo as part of the children's animal care training. She reassured the keeper that, although the children were young from a boarding school, the children were very advanced in animal communication and interaction.

Beth went on to suggest that the children had recently lost their own parents and thought that they may be able to comfort the little bear, if the keeper would allow them to get closer.

The keeper, after some thought, explained that she was just about to feed Snowflake and that they could accompany her.

Naturally the children were very excited about meeting Snowflake but Gwendoline, who was desperate for a cup of tea, told them that she would see them in the Zoo Café when they had finished feeding the little bear.

FORTY-SIX

THE LOGAN BROTHERS OBSERVATIONS

Meanwhile, back in the Zoo car park, the Logan brothers had completed maintenance checks on the transporter and had settled down to read the days newspapers when Liam recognised an old white Ford Popular in the car park.

"Brandon, isn't that the car that appeared to be following us when we initially set out for the zoo?"

"It looks like it. It's not exactly a car you can forget, compared to all these other newer cars in the car park".

"Yes. Strange though, you wouldn't expect a car of that age to still be safe on the road. Obviously somebody has looked after it really well and it has probably been

177

garaged. Have you got your binoculars, I've lent mine to the children?"

Liam had a good look at the car through the binoculars and then around the car park, which was by now quite full. "Oh, that's interesting; if you look, one, two, three, four cars to the right of the Ford Popular, you will see our friend Winston in the blue Escort looking at us!"

"Are you sure he's looking at us, he appears to have his back to us!"

"Yes, but with the binoculars you can see his image in the mirror is reflected back at us!"

"Great, what do you suggest we do? Ignore him?" said Brandon looking to his older brother for inspiration.

"Never ignore a potential problem, my Viriddion sibling. I suggest we carry on doing what we intended to do ... read the papers ... ... and telephone Rubin McDonald with that Ford Popular's number plate to see who it is registered to".

Meanwhile, in the blue car, Winston of course had no intention of ignoring them. He and his wife purposefully set out to follow the drivers and the children today. He had encouraged his wife to keep an eye on the children, while he spied on the drivers.

Winston's heart had sunk when he saw it was the Zoo they were visiting, as he didn't like the idea of being surrounded by frantic kids again.

He was therefore silently relieved that he didn't have to tour around a Zoo for the day with his wife. Not that he didn't want to spend time with her but the work promotion that he would be in line for, by reporting the release of Santa and making a citizen's arrest of the real Bank robbers, was far more important for him at the moment.

FORTY-SEVEN

TIME WITH SNOWFLAKE

Back at the Polar Bear enclosure, the Zoo Keeper knew that it wasn't the usual protocol to allow strangers to go near new admissions until they had finished their usual well-being assessments.

However, when she heard the children's request via their animal care tutors Beth and Luke, she felt empathy for the children. She found herself remembering how she longed to touch and care for the animals when she was doing her animal care training and never forgot the people who gave her those first opportunities.

So the keeper brought Snowflake a bucket of fish and allowed the four children to stand quietly in the corner to watch. Beth and Luke remained at the door.

As the keeper tried to offer some fish to Snowflake, Snowflake backed away into the corner with her head low to the ground, continually crying, as Snow had described it.

After a while, the keeper began to think it might be best to leave the little bear with the fish to eat undisturbed, and turned to suggest to the children that they leave and watch from a lower window in another room, when she noticed the four of them were kneeling on the floor crying.

Albeit their crying was quiet compared to the little bear, she turned to speak to their tutors Beth and Luke. She began to explain that, it probably wasn't a good time for the bear and obviously too emotional and painful for the children, possibly due to the loss of their parents recently, when she suddenly became aware that Snowflake and the children had all stopped crying.

When she turned around to the children again, she found Snowflake lying on the ground with the children, stroking and quietly talking to her.

Rachael, the keeper, backed away alongside Beth and Luke and looked on with tears in her eyes, as the children slowly began to feed Snowflake her fish dish.

FORTY-EIGHT

ERNIE AND ALFIE -V- OFFICER GWENDOLINE STIRWELL-TWINE

The two off duty elves, one dressed as a school boy and the other as his Father, had found themselves in the Zoo Café, after Alfie had frantically cleaned off the mud that tiger had thrown at him.

They had returned pretty sharp quick to where the children were but had discovered that Snow was no longer carrying her large bag but that it was being carried by a strange lady whom had joined the children. They had seen the lady before with the children but couldn't understand how she had managed to get the bag off Snow when they couldn't.

Nevertheless, they weren't ones to give up on their endeavour to retrieve the bank notes that they had hidden in a Christmas present, they thought Snow had in her bag.

Still believing that the present was in the bag, they followed the lady who was now carrying Snow's bag. They had followed her down and around to the Polar Bears enclosure and now they were sitting behind her in the Café.

The bag was close to Alfie but the Café was so full of people that he had to be careful. He looked around to see if anyone was watching him and, when he saw Ernie give him the nod, he went to place his hand, yet again, into the bag that was hanging over the lady's shoulder.

But, right at that time, Gwendoline took the bag off her shoulder and placed it on the table in front of her, much to the annoyance of the off duty elves.

Alfie and Ernie looked on despondently, as Gwendoline carried on drinking her cup of tea with her right hand and with her left hand she ran her fingers over the colourful embroidered bag.

"Beautiful" she thought. And: then after looking around to check that the children were not in sight, she began to empty out the content of the bag on the table.

Alfrie and Ernie could not believe what they were seeing and were going to great lengths not to miss anything by standing up, peering round her shoulders, fending off other table hunters who may have thought that the gentleman and his boy was leaving because they had got up.

Out came a white jumper with a colourful bobble hood, a large sketchbook with a Polar Bear and Slender Loris on the front, a beautifully embroidered long purse that matched her bag, a couple of pencils and a rubber, a half-eaten apple and ... ... that was it.

The two off duty elves looked absolutely stunned. "Ernie, it's not in her bag!"

"No. That means it must be back in their log cabin. Come on, no time to loose. We've got to get going while they're still here.

However, in the Zoo car park, the Logan brothers had just received a call on their mobile phone from Rubin. He had told them that the old white Ford Popular was registered to a David Seymour in Finland.

"What's Seymour's car doing in the car park, Liam?"

"I don't know, but I think we're about to find out whose driving it" and handed the binoculars to Brandon to look at a gentleman and child hurriedly getting into the car.

"Who are they? Hang on Liam, do you see the school uniform the boy's wearing?" passing the binoculars back to his brother.

"It's the Viridis Junior University uniform with the Viridis symbol on the top pocket. Well we can't follow them because we can't leave the children here. At least we know where the car is headed back to. We'll catch up with it later. The children will be out soon".

FORTY-NINE

GWENDOLINE STIRWELL-TWINE

Gwendoline thought, by looking through Snow's bag, she might find out more about the children and where they had come from. She looked for the garment label in the jumper and found none, yet it looked far too good to be home knitted. There was no label in the bag but, then Snow had said that her Mother had made it.

The sketchbook contained free hand sketches. On the front cover was a picture of a Polar Bear and the face of a Slender Loris. On the back, there was nothing except two small symbols at the bottom of the page.

Gwendoline did not recognise the symbols at the bottom of the page but continued to flip her way through the sketchbook noticing a boy that looked like one of the twin boys up a tree holding a lion cub … … and a fully grown tiger with large areas of torn fur with a cub leaning on its back ....

Gwendoline quickly closed the book and placed the objects including the half eaten apple back in the bag as she heard the children approaching.

On the children's arrival at the Café, Snow made straight for Gwendoline and began excitedly telling her about the poor little cub called Snowflake.

"That sounds like a really sad story Snow but I must be going. Winston will be expecting me", she handed Snow her bag back and disappeared out of the Café.

"Yes, and we must be going too. Liam and Brandon will be wondering where we've got to", reminded Beth.

Once settled back in the carrier Beth handed Lemmie back to Snow but could see that Snow was anxious about something as she kept moving things in and out of her bag.

"What's up Snow?"

"The things in my bag are all out of order, I must get them right again before I put Lemmie and Loppie back in".

Beth looked at Luke and Luke returned her concerned look.

FIFTY

VILLAGE POLICE STATION

In the Lapland village police station, Inspector Moody was getting a little concerned. He had spent some time with David Seymour the Santa they had in custody and he was beginning to like him.

Inspector Moody just couldn't find a motive for a person like Seymour to carry out such a bank robbery, particular as he lived in the village and had been a Lapland Santa for a few years now but, the bank insurance company were insistent on putting him in front of a jury.

Only yesterday, Inspector Moody had reminded the other officers' that the reporter, Winston Stirwell, should not be allowed to visit Seymour because he just didn't believe him, when he said that he was a private detective on Santa's side.

Meanwhile, David Seymour had spent a lot of time

thinking, whilst in custody. Thinking about things that he had put to the back of his mind while he was busy preparing a safe place for his son Michael and his Viriddion family to stay when they visited Earth again.

He had thought about the time when his Viriddion wife Minal, well at least that was what he called her because he couldn't ever pronounce her Viriddion name, and his daughter May had died. They had been on a mission with two other biologist on Viridis, taking samples of the scorched earth at the rim of an unsteady volcano, when it erupted and they were caught in the direct first flow.

So when it was decided by the Viridis Counsel to send out Viridis 6000 to Earth, with E-Contacts to prepare the way for Viridis 6000 to then return to Earth again about ten years later, he thought the loss of his wife and daughter would not be so painful, if he was preparing a place for his son Michael and his family.

David Seymour began to think of the cottage in the village, where he had slowly been able to put family pictures up of himself, Minal, Michael and May. He smiled to himself, as he remembered Michael and May in their Viriddion Junior University uniforms and then his smiled disappeared, as he began to imagine the mess of the cottage that Ernest Pratt and Alfred Pike might be making.

David Seymour was looking forward to bringing his family to Earth; however an incident which occurred about five years ago had caused him to rethink about whether or not his family would be safe on Earth.

Whilst playing the Santa role, he was visited by a child and Mother who wore fur coats, made from a mixture of real animal furs. The Mother had torn her coat on a sleigh when she was climbing out of it but her husband had reassured her that she wasn't to worry because he could easily obtain another one.

That incident had caused David Seymour to carry out further investigations, as he had previous knowledge about how such fur was made and who must had made it. But: he wasn't aware that the Yapikus had contacts on Earth.

He then received a message via his E-Contact equipment, warning him to stop Viridis 6000 from landing and, not knowing who to trust, he stopped his contacts with the Viridis Counsel. He, of course, became very scared for his son and any Viriddions' visiting or hoping to make their home on Earth.

FIFTY-ONE

ERNIE AND ALFIE

Back in the log cabin, whilst eating her supper, Snow was informing Liam and Brandon about the visit to the Zoo. She told them about the sea lions, Samson the tiger, Snowflake the polar bear and the boy who kept following her about.

"What did the boy look like, Snow?" enquired Liam.

"He wore a school uniform, just like the uniforms we wore, if we visited the University Ship. Do you think he was from Viridis?"

"No, I don't think so but, I think he knows someone who is!"

"Liam, if it's one of the two men that Santa mentioned, why would they be following Snow around?" questioned Brandon.

Beth then mentioned to the Logan brothers about

Gwendoline joining them and volunteering to look after Snow's bag and, Snow saying that the objects in her bag were not in their usual position when Gwendoline returned the bag to her.

"This gets stranger by the minute but, it ties up with her husband spying on us in the car park. I think we need to keep Gwendoline and her husband at arm's length. We've only got a couple of days left before we return to the ship".

Ernest Pratt and Alfred Pike, were definitely the two off duty elves, which David Seymour referred the Logan brothers to, when they visited him in police custody and, they were definitely the two dressed up as the gentleman and young boy which the Logan brothers had seen drive off in David Seymour's white Ford Popular from the Zoo car park.

Meanwhile, they had decided that it was not a good time to search the log cabin again and would have to wait until they had more time, as they were due back on duty wrapping more presents, for the temporary Santa.

On returning to the cottage, they had quickly garaged David Seymour's car and were busy removing their disguises and stuffing them back in the large box where they found them, when Ernest thought he heard a buzzing noise come from the lounge and so went to investigate it.

"Alfred, you plugged the sewing machine in, not the heater. I told you to turn the heater on. Now turn it off because we'll be late for work!"

"I had a lot on my mind. We only have a couple of days left. If we don't get that present back from the little girl before she opens it, we're in deep trouble. If she opens it and shows her drivers, they'll take it to the police and the police will have us arrested because they know that we are the elves who wrapped those presents up. Everyone knows that Santa doesn't wrap his own presents!"

"I'll have to put my thinking cap on then, wont I?" frowned Ernest.

"Hey Ernie: why should a sewing machine make a buzzing noise when it's switched on?"

"What do I care? All I know is, when we leave this place, we need to take that machine with us and give it to the boss man. Well that was the deal in exchange for the bank information. Goodness knows what the boss man wants with an old sewing machine".

FIFTY-TWO

CAPTAIN GENESIS

Back on the Viridis 6000, Captain Genesis had called counsel. His concern was for the children and he had received some unsettling information from Roger in the Intelligence Unit.

Roger had reported that the American UFO unit had received a message from their Officer Gwendoline Stirwell-Twine, asking her boss for the meaning of a particular sign that she had not seen before. The sign, as she described it, was a round circle positioned between the north and west points of a five pointed star.

Apparently, the Officer said that she had seen this sign on the back of one of the children's drawing books and, as usual, one of her colleagues laughed at her find and suggested that her marriage had finally come back to earth because her signs in the sky were now turning to signs on paper.

But, the E-Contact had suggested that a hieroglyphics translator be brought in to decipher the sign.

The Officer had also reported that the particular drawing book had a sketch in it of a young boy sitting up a tree holding a lion cub and a tiger with large wounds over its back.

"Hmm that's disturbing" responded the Captain.

"Well they're wasting their money on a translator" continued Roger, "it doesn't take a genius to work out that a circle could represent the Sun; any Egyptian can tell you that. At least we know Snow's busy with her memory sketching and the children are busy with their tasks".

"Yes I agree but, I'm more concerned about our E-Contact's suggestion. What's he playing at?"

"It could just be he's trying to waste their time or keep them occupied because, as you know the sign is meaningless on its own.

"Maybe and what's that Officer doing looking at Snow's sketchbook. How did she get hold of it?" sighed Captain Genesis as he rested back on his chair, in deep thought. "I feel very uneasy about our E-Contact. Can you look back over his contacts and into his movements over the past few years Roger?"

Yes, Captain Genesis was very worried and getting more worried by the day for the children., as he looked around the counsel table at the young unit members proudly sitting listening to him relay the latest news he had heard from the Intelligence Unit.

He could have contacted them through their Visionars,

after all they were seen to be using them a lot lately, as they desperately sought knowledge, guidance and strength from their ancestors and recently lost parents. However, Captain Genesis felt he needed to talk to them directly.

The population of the Viridis 6000 was now only forty, with just over half under the age of fourteen. He even had to leave Louis, who was only fourteen, in charge of the bridge whilst he held counsel.

They needed to know the facts. That: the appearance of the Yapikus, could mean that, Earth would need a lot of help to be rid of an invasion by them; there appeared to be an American Agent who is suspicious of the children, which could cause the arrest of the children; and, it also appeared that one of the E-Contacts in the American UFO departments was working against the Viriddions'.

Captain Genesis had obviously reminded them that, whilst they were under the ice in the Atlantic, no contact could be made directly with them, either from the children or an E-Contact because, such a contact could alert Earth Intelligence to their position.

Therefore, they had to wait for the children to return to get the full facts. That's if they managed to get back.

They would then have to make some urgent decisions in case Viridis 6000's atmospheric system should fail. He wanted the members of counsel to consider three questions. Firstly, should the Viridis 6000 leave planet Earth and look for another planet to settle on? Secondly, should all those that are left on Viridis 6000 go to the surface and make their individual ways on Earth? Or thirdly, everyone goes to the surface and stays together?

Of course, these questions were not new to any member

of the Viridis 6000, however old or young and Old Ridoros had been thinking about those questions since counsel decided to return to Earth.

He had not expected to live so long and, if the ships physicians hadn't worked out why he had out lived the illness on the ship, he had. Old Ridoros was convinced that it was due to the atmospheric changes in the ship.

On the other hand because he had always preferred working in the field, it may have had nothing to do with the atmospheric changes. But, if it was, then he feared he could never leave the ship because his lungs would not re-adapt to Earth atmospheric pressure again.

FIFTY-THREE

OFFICER GWENDOLINE STIRWELL-TWINE

When Gwendoline Stirwell-Twine awoke the following morning, she was a little dis-pleased that Winston had not been home and that she had spent the night on her own but she knew he was doing a very important job, especially since she had just received word from one of her colleagues back in the UFO department.

So when he did arrive just when she was making her own breakfast, she quickly laid up the breakfast table with his usual boiled egg and bread fingers.

"Winston, I've had a call from my office to say that we were not to let the visiting children out of our sight", said Gwendoline peering around the paper Winston was reading. "My colleague said that he couldn't tell me anymore, whilst I wasn't in the office but, that I needed to report to him daily regarding where they were and what they were doing.

"Oh really! And what do you think I've been doing all night in the car, playing tiddlywinks with frozen spiders!" muttered a very tired Winston.

"Sorry love, I didn't mean you hadn't been working all night. You get yourself into bed and I'll keep my eye on them throughout the day."

"Thanks dear, any news on the space ship they did find?"

"My colleague says that the governments are still arguing between themselves about whether to blow it up but he has suggested that they should just leave it, as it could be a decoy to distract intelligence from the real aliens that arrived in the UFO I saw, when we were on honeymoon. Remember?" She peered again around the newspaper to see whether he was listening.

As she did so, she noticed a column that read "... tigers found with wounds in India ... much improved. ...". "No, surely not" Gwendoline's mind reflected back to the sketch she had seen in Snow's book. "They couldn't have been to India and back", she thought as she began to collect the dirty dishes up from the table.

FIFTY-FOUR

SNOW'S SKETCHES

Meanwhile, Snow and the children were coming to terms with the fact that they only had two days left before returning to the Viridis 6000. They thought that they would spend this day catching up with their notes and around the village and their last day, being Christmas Eve, up on the ski slopes.

Snow looked upon the cover of her sketchbook. A few tears came to her eyes, as she looked once again upon her family room on Viridis 6000 and her beautiful Mother. But, as she flipped through the sketchbook her tears slowly dried as she remembered drawing the field with Old Ridoros feeding some hens; her friend Lemmie; her best E-Friend Penny; the old Doe who saved her; a tiger with wounds and her cub; George up tree with cub; one empty page; another empty page; and Yapikus ship.

"So why did I leave some empty pages? Oh, I know", thought Snow, as she took out her pencil and quickly sketched the multi-transporter in its role as a helicopter with ropes falling to the ground.

Then, after another little thought, on the next page, she quickly sketched the helicopter again with Liam and Brandon laying asleep under it, as she smiled to herself remembering the scene back in Africa.

Snow then looked at her sketch of the Yapikus ship and she shuddered at the cruelness of the pods as they dragged the fur off the animals. She began to wonder whether Snowflakes Mother had been a victim of the pods and began to sketch Snowflake the young cub they had managed to get feeding in the Zoo.

"Snow, are you coming to the village", asked Beth as she peered at the sketch Snow was just finishing. "Can I have a little look in your sketchbook Snow?"

"Ok Beth, but don't tell Liam and Brandon", implying a shyness to having her work looked at.

Beth flipped through the sketchbook and although she told Snow that the sketches were very good, an awful feeling came over her as she saw Snow put the sketchbook back in her bag. Beth began to imagine what Gwendoline may have seen, if she had looked into her bag, whilst she looked after it for a while at the Zoo.

It wasn't long after that, that the Viriddion visitors were walking around the Lapland village, perhaps for the last time. Beth had agreed that they could buy something to take back to the ship with the money that Rubin, the E-Contact in Scotland, provided them with for their trip to Lapland.

Liam and Brandon had walked to the village with them but then left them and said they would meet again later in the Café.

So Jimmy and George had made for their favourite shop window full of model ships, sports cars and an aeroplane. Beth found herself accompanying Tayla and Snow to the material shop. Just as the boys loved to make models the girls loved to put different materials together and make their own clothes and Beth was no different.

Luke, well he wasn't sure where he should be. He knew he needed to keep his eyes on the twins because he knew if he didn't they would finish up buying a truck load of models but, on the other hand, he would have loved to see the material that Beth would have chosen, so he could have gone in and bought it for her.

So while Luke was hovering between the model shop and the material shop, Beth was hovering over two different material colours. When Beth had seen the fine brushed velvet in the window at the beginning of the stay in Lapland, she thought she knew the exact colour she would buy but, now she found she was beginning to question her own choice and wondering whether Luke would like the colour she chose.

Tayla and Snow had already made up their minds, what material they were going for and disappeared ahead of her into the shop. Beth wondered whether she could just ask Luke, what he thought of the colours but he had gone into the shop with the boys. On turning, she caught sight of Gwendoline approaching them and her heart began to beat faster.

"Hi Beth, last minute holiday shopping. Need any help?"

"Yes we're going home tomorrow and No, I'm fine thank you. I'm just giving the girls a little space", responded Beth anxiously. She hadn't intended to stay outside but she didn't want Gwendoline to be left alone with them and if she were to go in now, she surmised that Gwendoline would have that time alone with them whilst she was being served.

"Where did you say you lived, Beth?"

"I'm not sure whether I did say but it's … …" Beth was beginning to feel very uneasy with the questions, so she put her hand on her wrist Vigil and pressed the top button. Within seconds Liam and Brandon appeared.

"Oh hi Gwendoline, no Winston today?" cheerfully asked Liam.

"No, no, he's picked up a chill and so he's staying in the warm today. I thought I'd do some last minute shopping too because we'll be leaving soon".

Soon after that, Luke and the children appeared from their shops and Liam invited Gwendoline to join them in the Café, as the children were after a hot chocolate drink. Gwendoline happily accepted but said that she would meet them there as she needed to pop into the material shop first.

Beth wasn't certain why Liam had invited Gwendoline to join them but she trusted him. She soon discovered Liam's intention when he ensured that Snow sat between Brandon and him. So when Gwendoline joined them, she could only find one seat available and that was between Liam and Luke.

Whilst sitting in the Café, chatting with the Viriddion visitors, Gwendoline's mobile phone went off and she popped out of the Café to answer it. When she returned she said that it was only her office wondering when she was coming back to work.

FIFTY-FIVE

CAPTAIN GENESIS

Meanwhile, back on Viridis 6000, Captain Genesis and his crew were sitting stunned and absolutely horrified at what they had just seen.

Roger and Sarah his daughter from the Intelligence Unit had brought to their attention an incident that was occurring around the UFO in Iceland that an American Agent had discovered. Over the past few days the American UFO Department had been in dialogue with various Presidents and governing bodies to determine how to deal with it.

Roger, had been able to monitor various discussions held in the American UFO Department and, although the Viriddions' recognised the space ship as a Yapikus Fur Collecting Ship, the UFO Department were, at least up until recently, prepared to leave the UFO alone to see whether it makes contact or someone comes out of it.

However, the recent monitoring of the American UFO Department and being able to see the UFO surrounded by military units, it appeared that it had been decided to send an unmanned probe to it. If they couldn't detect anything living within it, they would blow it up.

The Captain and his crew had sat hypnotised in silence, as they watched the probe approach the ship, then being withdrawn and the ship finally being blown up.

Captain Genesis rested back on his chair. He glanced around at the crew and his Grandfather, Old Ridoros. The reality of what could happen to them and their ship, presently positioned under the ice in the Atlantic if it was discovered by the Earth Governments, cut deep in the pit of his stomach.

Sarah, Roger's daughter, sensing the Captain's distress, walked around beside him. She wanted to put her hand on him to console and reassure him that all would be well but, she remained still.

Captain Genesis sensed Sarah's nearness and felt comforted but, he had been thinking a lot lately about the Viriddions' present home under the ice. Thinking about what would happen to Viridis 6000 if the Viriddions' did decide to settle on Earth and whether he would be able to leave his ship for the Government to find and possibly blow up.

Old Ridoros also sensed the thoughts that must have been going through his Grandson's mind and in true Viriddion style he took the Captain's left hand in his right hand and brought it up across his chest to his right shoulder, securing it in position by enclosing the Captain's hand with his other hand. "Grandson, I know you will know what to do, when the time comes. Go and put your Visionars on for a while".

Old Ridoros left to go back to the field. As he left the bridge he caught a glimpse of his Grandson holding out his hand to Sarah who was still standing beside him, and he smiled to himself.

FIFTY-SIX

ERNIE AND ALFIE

Meanwhile, whilst the Viriddion visitors were spending a few hours in the Lapland village, the off duty elves, Ernie and Alfie were busy visiting the children's log cabin once again.

They were up early that morning, observing the cabin and when they saw the visitors leave for the village, they knew that this had to be their last chance to find the little girls present.

The elves were very good at breaking into places and so it didn't take them long to open the cabin door to let in themselves. As usual, everything was so neat and tidy, Ernie gave Alfie strict instructions, this time, to replace things exactly as he found them, otherwise the children will know that someone has been looking around their cabin.

The elves looked in beds, under beds, in cupboards, in the cooker, in the fringe, in the bin, in bags but they found nothing that looked like a present or a white bank bag that might have held the bank notes.

Of course, Snow's bag was not in the cabin but, they knew it wasn't in there anyway, since that lady had emptied Snow's bag in the Zoo Café.

"I know Alfie, it must be in the garage".

"Good thinking Ernie", replied Alfie as he made his way to the garage through the inner door from the lounge area. "Wow, gosh this carrier is whopping when you get up close to it".

"Yes, now be careful how you go around it. Don't go scratching it, it might set off an alarm!"

"Ernie, the present could be in the carrier!"

"Don't be an idiot. Why would the men be looking after a Christmas present?"

"Just a thought! Well there is nothing else in this garage other than the carrier, so are we're leaving?"

Just as Alfie asked the question, he lost his footing on the step to the inner door and fell back against the carrier. In fear, the off duty elves froze on the spot waiting for an alarm to sound but, nothing!

"Ernie, no alarm. Do you think you could gently break into the carrier?"

Ernie did exactly that. He fiddled about with a few keys and opened the driver's door. Both of the elves slowly stepped up and sat in the two front seats.

"Cor Ernie, look at these dials, you'd need to be a pilot to drive this!"

Alfie, placed a helmet on and put some goggles on and then pretended he was in a racing car. Ernie seeing some binoculars looked through them and when he focused them on Alfie, he pretended he had been frightened by the face he saw.

"Oh very funny Ernie. Actually, this is some very serious equipment here. It must be worth a fortune! We could take this ..."

"No. It's all for show. It's what they do in Hollywood. Those drivers must be charging that family a fortune to ferry them around, so they have to spruce the carrier up to look as if they're getting their monies worth".

Just then the two drivers appeared either side of them.

"Find what you're looking for gentlemen?" questioned Liam with a very serious voice.

"Oh sorry. We were just passing ... ... and we saw the door open ... ... and we couldn't help but have a look ... ... lovely car ... ..."shook and stammered Ernie, whilst Alfie struggled to get his helmet and goggles off.

"And, that's why we have a silent alarm fitted, so we can catch burglars like you and not just frighten them away", joined in Brandon.

The Logan brothers brought Ernie and Alfie into the lounge area and Liam suggested to them that he should call the police. The off duty elves pleaded with them that they had no intention of stealing anything that didn't belong to them but tried to say that they should be keeping an eye on the chap who is acting as a private detective for the Santa in custody.

They had gone on to explain that they had seen the

detective spying on their log cabin throughout the night. Liam questioned them, as to how they knew that, and they said they had been passing on their way home from their shift after wrapping presents during the night.

Of course, Liam and Brandon knew that Santa's grotto was in the complete opposite direction to the log cabin but they weren't going to let on that they knew that they weren't exactly telling the truth because, it so happened, they did believe them in relation to Winston Stirwell.

When Liam asked them whether they were the Ernest Pratt and Alfred Pike that are staying in David Seymour's collage in the village, they looked a little surprised that the drivers should know who they were but, they didn't deny it.

Liam knew that he would have to go very gently on the two off duty elves, especially as they could be seen as witnesses' against Santa, in his coming court case. So the Logan brothers sent them on their way, feeling fairly confident that whatever antics they were up to, they wouldn't carry them on any more.

When the children arrived back, Liam and Brandon informed them about the Ernest Pratt and Alfred Pike episode but, reassured them that he didn't think they were the real problem.

FIFTY-SEVEN

THROW A SNOW MISSILE AND SHOUT "SET SANTA FREE"

The Logan brothers were more concerned about Winston Stirwell and his wife Gwendoline's interest in the children. They had planned to fly back to Rubin in Scotland, who had sent them an urgent text message to say he had something for them that might help David Seymour, but that they would have to collect it.

This meant that they would have to leave the children although they would have Beth and Luke with them. However, if the off duty elves had seen Winston spying on them during the night, they would have to leave for Scotland almost immediately whilst it was still day time, so Winston didn't see them leave.

The Logan brothers explained about the instructions

they had received from the E-Contact Rubin McDonald and suggested that if Beth, Luke and the children walked up to the village and started to play snow missiles at each other, Gwendoline would not notice the carrier leaving with the drivers in and therefore, when Winston did his usual spying during the night he hopefully would presume all of them were in the log cabin.

Beth was a little concerned that the Logan brothers would not be there for them in an emergency but they reassured her that the quicker they went, the quicker they would return. Before leaving, Brandon gave the Christmas present, which he had been looking after in the Carrier, back to her. He had explained to Snow that they may not be able to get back by Christmas Day, so it was important for her to open her present from Santa, even if they hadn't returned.

Snow had attempted to persuade Brandon not to go and suggested that Liam would be all right on his own but Beth had reminded Snow that Liam would need a co-pilot for the distance he would be travelling and help with conversion of the carrier to a helicopter. Meanwhile, Liam, sensing the little six year olds anxiety, had promised Snow that he would try and get Brandon back to collect them by Christmas Day.

Therefore according to their instructions, Beth, Luke and the children walked back up to the village and when they reached the village Jimmy and George had no problem in throwing the first snow missiles. Tayla and Snow soon joined in just as forcefully, laughing and screaming with delight when they made contact.

It was late afternoon on the day before Christmas Eve.

The failing sun light was being replaced by all manner of sparkling lights from the village shop windows and village Christmas tree outside the police station. The children found themselves being caught up with other children gathering together chanting "Set Santa free. Set Santa free".

Not surprisingly, it wasn't long before Beth, Luke and the children began chanting "Set Santa Free", as they continued to play snow missiles. Within a short time the children who had originally come to protest were joining in the snow missiles game with the Viriddion visitors. The game being, to throw a snow missile and shout "Set Santa Free".

Beth and Luke appeared to be enjoying the moment, targeting one another even though they had their eyes peeled for Gwendoline and sure enough, they had seen her up at a window overlooking the village police station.

Similarly, Gwendoline had seen them and was encouraging her husband Winston to have another warm drink before starting his night spying on the children's log cabin, pointing out that the children were right there outside their window, playing with the snow.

"Yes but, where are the drivers. Are they playing with the snow?"

"I can't see them but they're usually sitting in that Café. If the children are there, then you can bet your bottom dollar that they're close to them. They never leave the children. So I'll keep an eye on the children and let you know when they leave".

Gwendoline was not the only person to see the children. Inspector Moody had heard them in the police station and was getting rather anxious over the fact that the chanting to "Set Santa Free" had started again. The last thing he and his men needed over Christmas was extra shifts, so he sent one of the officers' out with some mince pies and sweets for the children, hoping that the children would keep their demonstration low key.

Inspector Moody had other things on his mind in relation to Santa. Just when he was beginning to believe David Seymour was innocent, he had received a telephone call from Winston Stirwell, the private detective alias newspaper reporter.

Winston had told him, he had seen two strange men, a bit rough looking, and hanging around David Seymour's cottage. He had confronted them, as to what they wanted and they had said that they were old friends of his. And, when Winston told them that Seymour was in custody, they said that they didn't know that and that they would call again later.

Winston had said that there was something suspicious about them and that they could have been the men who Seymour intended to pass the stolen bank money onto. Of course, Winston had only given Inspector Moody the information on the basis that if there was a story in it, Inspector Moody would have to give him first option to print it.

Following that information, Inspector Moody had felt he had no option but to question David Seymour about the two characters that had allegedly visited his cottage but David Seymour had just sat and listened and made no comment.

For Inspector Moody, making no comment was a sign

of guilt which had disappointed him. And, when he gave him the benefit of the doubt, asking him whether he had any enemies, suggesting he may have been set up, David Seymour said that as he was trained as a Veterinarian, he was bound to have reported people for animal cruelty to the authorities over the years.

David Seymour had sat in silence as if he didn't want to make any comment but, it wasn't because he didn't want to make comment, he just didn't know where to begin and, in any event, he couldn't think how the appearance of the two strange characters had anything to do with the robbery of the village bank.

In fact, he was absolutely convinced it was the continuation of the fur coat incident which resulted in him making enquiries about the family and finding out the husband's contact for buying fur coats and then confronting the seller in his large property set within high iron gates and beautifully maintained grounds.

David Seymour had wondered what would become of the confrontation he had with the seller, after he threatened that he would report him to the authorities if he didn't say how he receives his fur coats but he was seen off the premises by a couple of rough characters.

It was after that occasion he had received a strange message via his Viridis E-Contact equipment, which had caused him to stop contact with Viridis but, it now looked like the seller of the fur coats wasn't happy with David Seymour knowing about his dealings in fur coats.

However, David Seymour was feeling a little relieved since Inspector Moody had let him know that the names of the two young men who visited him in custody, were

Liam and Brandon Logan. He remembered that at the time of the visit, he was very uncertain about trusting even a Viriddion visitor but those two young men, he presumed, had to be related to old James Logan, the E-Contact in Scotland and therefore he had great faith in them resolving the predicament he had now found himself in.

Meanwhile, outside the police station, the mince pies and sweets were going down well and the demonstrations were becoming very low key. Even one of the off duty elves threw a snow missile, shouted "Set Santa Free" and grabbed a mince pie before being dragged off by the other off duty elf.

"Alfie, what are you doing shouting "Set Santa Free"?"

"At least I got a mince pie out of it. You, still haven't come up with any more ideas about how to get that present before the little one opens it" cheekily retaliated Alfie.

"Well tomorrow is Christmas Eve and the last day to get it. So relax, I'll think of something" hissed Ernie cuffing Alfie around the ear.

FIFTY-EIGHT

CAPTAIN GENESIS

Since the Yapikus Ship was blown up in Iceland, the Russian and American ships had returned to their usual surveillance of the North Atlantic Ocean and the Viridis 6000 had picked them up on their radar on several occasions. Although they had not come within the Russian and American radar range, the crew had to keep alert to the possibility of being seen and so Louis with other young crew members were busy on the bridge with Captain Genesis.

Roger Baker and Sarah his daughter, in Intelligence Unit on the Viridis 6000, were also kept busy looking for more Yapikus ships because Old Ridoros was convinced that the Yapikus would not just send one or two ships at a time.

They had also been reviewing the American E-Contact's

messages to Viridis. Roger had reported that messages were regular; except up until a year ago, when although the contacts continued they appeared very repetitive.

"What do you mean, repetitive. How can a message be repetitive? Do you mean he literally sent the same message over and over again?" queried Captain Genesis.

"I mean that when he sent one message followed by another a month later, it was the same message with the same words, same tone, same pauses, as the message that he been previously sent!"

"Why would he do that?"

"From what we can surmise" said Roger bringing Sarah into the conversation "he must have recorded a message to send on occasions if he hadn't anything new to report..."

"... or he's reading a set piece but, in any event the messages are definitely sent from Joseph Montgomery because the system recognises his voice" continued Sarah.

"This is really exasperating. We can't attempt to contact Montgomery whilst we're under the ice. Contact would clearly pin point our position to anyone interested in us. We can't even send Liam and Brandon a message to warn them of the dangers they could be in, from that Officer Stirwell-Twine", sighed Captain Genesis.

A movement at one of the ships portals caught his attention. The ships portals were often a point of attraction and entertainment for the young crew by the variety of sea life in their feeding or social behaviours. This time it was a beautifully lit up jelly fish. It had splayed out all of its tentacles over the portal, obviously feeding off tiny plankton on the portal, and it looked as if another jelly fish was attempting to release its tentacles from the portal to have the plankton for itself - not very successfully.

The sight of the two jelly fish brought a smile to the Captain's worried face. They were only two very small living creatures but they were feeding off even smaller creatures and the vulnerability of the plankton being wiped out by larger creatures reminded him of the importance of his ship's visit.

The occupants on his ship really only had one mission and that was to move from a dying planet. A planet, which was once similar to the planet Earth with large land areas of lush vegetation, trees and large oceans to support all manner of animals, but whose climate had changed causing the land and oceans to dry up and forcing every living thing to move underground from the heat.

Captain Genesis thought of Beth and the children and how they must be enjoying the surface of Earth, feeling the wind, rain and snow and touching and talking to animals in contrast to experiencing them only on the Visionars.

Of course, even he had not felt the weather phenomena as on Earth, or even as it once was on Viridis, but his Grandfather, Old Ridoros, had demonstrated the effects of surface weathers with the propellers on his model aeroplane and flicking water over him from the pond, whilst visiting him as a child in the Viridis 6000 field.

FIFTY-NINE

VIRIDDION ZIGZAG

When Snow awoke, the following morning, she looked at the date on her wrist vigil. "Yes" she excitedly shouted to herself. Today was Christmas Eve, the day before Christmas Day and only one day to go before she could open her present from Santa.

Snow took the brightly wrapped present out of her large bag. She hadn't handled the present since the day after Santa gave it to her because she had asked Brandon to give it back to Santa. She had thought it was the present which he had given her that had caused him to be accused of breaking in the village Bank.

However, Brandon had not returned it at that time, to give Snow time to change her mind about returning it to Santa but, because he had gone to visit Rubin, and didn't know whether he would be back before Christmas day, he had returned it to her.

"Do you think I should just have a peep", she asked Lemmie, as she gently brought him out of her bag clutching the soft fabric rabbit her Mother had made her when she was first born. His ears were made of soft lilac velvet, which Snow still stroked against her cheek when she was tired or upside and, just like Lemmie, Loppie was always kept very close to her, in her bag.

"I know, I know, I shouldn't peep so I shan't. We've got a busy day today. Liam and Brandon are away, so Jimmy and George want us to play ZigZag and then go skiing again. So you had better hang on tight to Loppie - you remember what happened last time, I nearly squashed you".

Snow carefully packed her bag and the Viriddion visitors were soon leaving the log cabin and walking via the village to the ski slopes which were alongside the play area, where the snow wasn't so deep.

The village was as busy as ever and, again the village children were gathering together and chanting "Set Santa Free".

Snow desperately wanted to stop and join in, as she wanted Santa to be free but Jimmy and George were too busy ahead of her deciding what programme they were going to play on their Vigil.

Tayla had caught sight of her long flowing red hair in the cake shop window and had stopped to tie it back, saying that it would get in the way when zigzagging.

Snow didn't want to bother Beth and Luke as their arms were linked and they appeared to be deep in discussion as they walked past the shops, so Snow ran up and pushed in between Jimmy and George.

"So what programme are we going for?" eagerly asked Snow.

"I think the team programme might be best because you haven't played it before have you Snow?"

"We could play boys against girls!" responded Jimmy.

So when they were all grouped together, they decided to set their wrist Vigils at the lowest team setting, as Beth suggested that it might be easiest for Snow. Jimmy and George began to give Snow a demonstration of how the Vigil works.

Jimmy and George between them explained that "... the aim of a team of players in Team Vigil ZigZag was to knock the lives off the opposite team players ... ... each player has nine lives ... ... each player needed to press the button marked "T" on their Vigils which will synchronise all Vigils on the same setting ... ... the Easy Play Setting chosen, means that they will get a knock out if the laser hits any part of the opponents arm that has the Vigil on ... For example, in the High Play Setting team members would only get a knock out if they managed to aim their laser directly on their opponents Vigil".

George lifted up his left arm and reminded them that, with the setting they had chosen, if the laser beam should fall on any part of his arm, he would lose a life. The contact would set off a bleeping sound signifying to both teams that he had lost a life.

"What should happen if I made contact with your arm and you made contact with my arm at the exact same time" asked Tayla, determined to grasp every move of the game.

"The Vigil will determine who had made contact closet to the Vigil and will only knock out the life of the player who made contact the furthest away" answered Jimmy.

"What if I lose all my lives, am I out the game", asked Snow, needing to clarify the possible situation.

"No. You are still part of the team because it is a tactical team game. If you work with one of your team members and arrange to get your Vigil in line between their Vigil and the opposition players Vigil, then you will get a life back when it knocks out a life of the opposition player" answered George as he demonstrated the situation by lining his Vigil up with Beth's and raising Snow's arm up into the middle of him and Beth's Vigil.

Luke reminded them of a few other rules, in relation to this particular programme, such as: players had to stay within ten metres from each other or their Vigils will start bleeping and could nullify the player's lives if the player stays outside the zone for too long; the Vigil is a non-respecter of player and therefore players in the same team as each other could knock out their own lives, in what could be called a home knock out; and, the Vigils could be put on "pause" for thirty seconds to promote tactic discussions.

The girls got together and discussed tactics. The boys got together as well and then the game began.

It looked as if the boys had made a decision to split up. Jimmy to concentrate on Beth, George on Snow and Luke on Tayla but, as the boys zigzagged about the girls, it looked as if the girls plans were to stay as a group and concentrate on one of the boys at a time, starting with Jimmy.

Jimmy soon shouted it wasn't fair and as he lost concentration his Vigil soon sounded, confirming he had lost a life. But, just as Jimmy's Vigil went off, so did Tayla's go off, as the result of a home knock out, making Jimmy feel much better.

The girls had another discussion and decided to stick to game plan and move on to Luke but not to surround him but keep in line, to avoid another home knock out.

The boys put their thumbs up, to indicate that they were sticking to their game plan and so the game continued.

The game was well on its way when they began to collect a few onlookers and Gwendoline was one of them. She had looked around for the two drivers but when she couldn't see them she presumed that they were very close and would appear quickly if the children needed them at any time.

Gwendoline watched the children zigzagging around each other, raising their wrists and lowering their wrist and then suddenly shouting "Yes" or "Pause". They appear to make no contact with each other unless they were grouping together after shouting "Pause".

Various questions were being expressed by the onlookers, such as: are they throwing something invisible? They look as if they are playing hockey or lacrosse without the sticks! Have they got some telepathic powers? And Gwendoline was having similar thoughts.

Gwendoline didn't like to see people do things that she didn't understand and the more she saw the more she was convinced that they were not human "How else could they explain the boy up the tree with a lion cub in his arms" she thought.

Gwendoline took her mobile phone out and dialled her office number. "Sir, this is Officer Stirwell-Twine. These children will be leaving in 24 hours, what am I meant to do? They are definitely not normal. I am watching them play a game in which they must have psychic powers?"

"Just don't let them leave your sight. They could be from the ship we've just destroyed but they mustn't get suspicious or they will go underground and we will lose them. I'll send our Military Intelligence Officer over".

SIXTY

OFFICER GWENDOLINE STIRWELL-TWINE

Snow had done her best but with only one life left, she was totally exhausted. She wondered whether she could voluntary give her last life away. She could see Gwendoline sitting over in the Café window and she began to feel thirsty and longed to sit down.

So when George finally knocked out her life she thanked him.

"Please Beth can I go and sit in the Café with Gwendoline and have a drink. I'll watch you from there?"

Beth felt a little unsure about the question proposed but agreed on the promise from Snow that she would alert her on the Vigil if she was at all uncertain about anything.

"Hi Snow, you look worn out, I'll get you a hot chocolate"

Snow flopped down on a chair at Gwendoline's table. Whilst she went off to get the hot chocolate, Gwendoline looked back at the child and knew that this may be the last opportunity she would get to discover more about the children, so she needed to be very careful how she questioned her.

When she returned to the table and gave Snow her drink, Gwendoline could see how tired she looked and allowed Snow to drink the hot chocolate in silence for a while.

"Snow you're exhausted".

"Beth said it's my lungs because they're new", replied Snow sipping away at her chocolate.

Gwendoline burst out laughing "And I suppose my lungs are old and that's why I would get exhausted if I was playing the game you were".

Snow couldn't quite see the funny side but smiled and kept sipping her drink.

"It looks a good game. Where did you learn it?" quizzed Gwendoline.

"Here. The twins taught it to me just now. It's on my Vigil" answered Snow drawing back her left sleeve and revealing her wrist Vigil.

"On your wrist watch?" questioned Gwendoline.

Snow noticed Gwendoline's mobile phone on the table beside her and replied "Yes. You have games on your mobile, I expect, and I've got a game on my watch".

"Oh yes, I have heard of that but I haven't seen one as yet. What are the other buttons for?"

"It's to let Beth or Luke know if I get lost. That's why we call it a Vigil".

"That's a very good idea; the schools should provide every child with a wrist Vigil, in this day and age".

"That reminds me", said Snow as she reached into her bag and drew out a small prettily wrapped parcel "I've got something for you. I'll give it to you now because you're a friend of mine and I might not have a chance to see you tomorrow but you mustn't open it until Christmas Day".

Gwendoline looked absolutely shocked and as she felt tears coming to her eyes for a few seconds she forgot her mission "Snow, you shouldn't have done that. You know you've made my holiday enjoyable. We will always be friends. Look I'll give you my mobile number and we can keep in touch".

Snow was pleased with that and was placing it in her bag when the others came into the Café, just as exhausted as Snow had been.

SIXTY-ONE

DAVID SEYMOUR - INSPECTOR MOODY - WINSTON STIRWELL - LOGAN BROTHERS

In custody, David Seymour, was getting a little anxious. He was normally a very busy person but finding himself with nothing to do in custody led him to think a lot.

For example, he was beginning to wonder why the Logan brothers had visited him and not his son Michael. After all, if the ship had returned then Michael and his family would have arrived. If that was the case, where were they?

Why had the Logan brothers not returned? Now that he knew who they were, he wanted to talk to them again and tell them more about those elves.

All this thinking was getting too much for Santa in

228

custody and even at night he was beginning to talk in his sleep. So much so, that Inspector Moody had placed an officer at his door with a tape recorder to record anything that might give his motive for robbery away whilst he slept.

However, David Seymour shouldn't have been that worried because the intensity of the chanting outside his police station was getting too much for Inspector Moody and even his wife had threatened to break Santa out of custody if her husband didn't.

As it happened, Inspector Moody had been making enquiries around the world about the names Ernest Pratt and Alfred Pike and he had recently received a message from an American Police Department stating the names Alfred Pike and Ernest Pratt were on their wanted list, apparently having robbed a bank before. So Inspector Moody had requested a picture of them and finger prints if they had them.

Despite the noise outside the police station, he was hopeful that the situation would be finished with very soon, including the constant telephoning from Winston Stirwell the journalist.

Winston Stirwell was not asleep today. Yes he had been awake all night, keeping an eye on the log cabin where the two drivers of the children were staying. It had been a quite night for him, which had given him time to think about how he could catch the drivers with the money Santa had stolen from the village bank.

Winston Stirwell had no evidence to date, of Santa robbing the village bank but he needed to justify to the kids, that you can't trust all Santa's. "After all", he thought "My Dad was a Santa and he was put in prison for stealing".

Therefore, if his wife was right, and the children would be leaving tomorrow, he had to move quickly if he wanted to get that story. So today, he was only having a quick kip and then he would be joining Gwendoline to see what those drivers were up to.

Unbeknown to Winston Stirwell, the Logan brothers were miles away back in Scotland, after receiving an urgent message from the Scotland E-Contact Rubin McDonald to collect something important that might help the David Seymour case.

On arriving, Rubin had shown them into a library with a wide bay window overlooking the west grounds. As the sun began to disappear below the tree line, Rubin turned the lights up and made the young men comfortable in front of a log fire, whilst Martha the housemaid made them welcome with cups of hot coffee and biscuits.

Rubin showed them pictures of two men they had definitely met before – Pratt and Pike. He provided a folder on them and allowed them to read it. The folder outlined the names of various banks they had broken into before and information on a prison where they had spent time. It also mentioned about a particular criminal gang that they were known to do work for, if it involved money.

The criminal gang were known for illegal fur trading. Rubin went on to explain that, according to the information he had received, that particular criminal gang had been under surveillance by a special task force for many years because they wanted to get the supplier. However, it is alleged that one of the gang, whilst detoxing from drugs in prison, kept shouting the word "Yapikus".

A recent intelligence review revealed that there was no real evidence to link this reference to the case and no new information over the past two years had stopped the progress of the undercover work.

The Logan brothers had sat back in silence for a while, contemplating the information they had heard and how relevant it was to them. They could, at least, now understand why Rubin couldn't explain everything over the phone.

SIXTY-TWO

SNOW'S CHASE

Back in Lapland on Christmas Eve Ernie and Alfie the off duty elves were busy. They had been told that they needed to work an additional shift during the day because the temporary Santa was mega busy. So Ernie and Alfie had decided that, in the short time they had left, they would find the children, kidnap Snow if necessary, and find out where her present is. They were not going to play at being happy helpful elves any more.

On their break they sought out the children finding them on the ski slopes. Snow had her usual big bag with her and she was going over particular moves with Gwendoline. They noticed that their teachers Beth and Luke were further down the slope and Tayla and the boys were in another group with some friends.

"Alfie, I'm going to work my usual Ernie charm and

offer that women some free lessons. She looks as if she could do with some. That's the only way we're going to get near Snow".

"Well rather you than me" groaned Alfie as he watched a delicate looking lady wobbling to keep her balance on skis that only seemed to be able to cross one over the other. "But then what? Snow will recognize me from the last time I tried to grab her. She'll never talk to me, especially because I broke her wrist watch".

"So that's how you get her to talk to you. While I'm busy with the lady, you offer the little one your watch to say sorry for frightening her and breaking her watch. When you've found out where the present is, signal to me and I'll come and help you get it".

So the off duty elves put their plan into action. Ernie was busy convincing Gwendoline she needed some lessons desperately and Alfie approached Snow.

Snow wasn't that convinced that the elf was sorry for frightening her earlier but the watch he offered her was different to hers and she thought it wouldn't do any harm to talk to him for a while. She was still a little tired from her morning playing Vigil ZigZag and went to sit for a rest on a nearby seat.

Alfie followed her and sat quietly beside her. Every now and then Alfie pointed to Gwendoline as one ski stepped on the other, causing her to roll over to one side. Snow and Alfie both laughed as Ernie ended up on his bottom when he tried to lift the posh lady up and she reacted defiantly pushing him away.

Alfie realised that time was getting on and he needed

to find out where that present was, so he gently began to ask a few questions. "Snow, I bet you're pleased you're going home soon?"

"Sure, but this snow is lovely. We don't have snow on Viridis".

"Sounds lovely and hot to me", smiled Alfie trying to keep the conversation going.

"Too hot, you can't play in it".

"When will you get to open your present, it might be something you can play with in the cool inside".

"I'm not meant to open it until tomorrow but I keep thinking about having a little peep under the paper", grinned Snow.

"Oh, I used to do that all the time. When I saw a present with my name on, I just had to have a peep before Christmas Day. Where is it Snow?"

"In my bag", answered Snow as she produced the present from her bag.

Alfie gasped in surprise, he wasn't really expecting Snow to produce it, just like that. In fact, he was so taken by surprise, he lost his balance on the tree trunk where they were sitting and fell backwards in the snow.

Snow laughed and laughed. She thought he looked so funny with his legs sticking in the air. Then it occurred to her that she shouldn't laughing at him and quickly put the present down on the snow to help Alfie back on his feet.

As Alfie got to his feet, Ernie joined them saying that the lady needed a break. Seeing the brightly wrapped red present with its large green ribbon on the ground he bent over and picked it up.

With Snow and Alfie back on the log, Ernie looked

at Alfie and Alfie looked at Ernie and then both of them looked at the present. The elves looked around them to make sure the rest of the children were still very busy.

"Ernie, Snow said she wanted just a little peep. You know, I bet you used to".

"Shall I just open the end very carefully then", said Ernie now getting a little impatient with Alfie. Ernie couldn't believe that Alfie had this present in his grasp and was making no effort to take it from Snow.

Before Snow could answer, Ernie had untied the present, pulled a white bank bag out, gave the paper and ribbon to Snow and sped off with Alfie in tow.

"No", cried Snow "That's my present from Santa. Come back!"

Snow folded the wrapping paper and ribbon into her bag, thinking that at least they hadn't taken that and then sped off after them, across the slopes, round some trees and up and down the snow banks. She could see them in front of her and they were not going to get away with her present.

Meanwhile, Beth and Luke were doing well coming to terms with the art of skiing. Beth had looked back for Snow and, although she couldn't see her she also couldn't see Gwendoline and therefore presumed she was possibly sitting in the Café again.

Tayla and the boys were still enjoying the ski slopes. They really were getting the hang of it and were making the most of their last few hours on the snow.

Gwendoline had seen Winston beckoning her and made an excuse to the elf that she needed a break. She had noticed that Snow was still with the other elf but she appeared happy and in any event "if she felt upset, she has her wrist Vigil with her", she thought.

It was about this time, that Inspector Moody and a couple of his officers were on their way to Santa's grotto. They hadn't visited the grotto in their police cars with the sirens blaring since they arrested David Seymour.

Inspector Moody had just received the pictures of Ernest Pratt and Alfred Pike and their finger prints and there was no doubt about it. Even if they hadn't taken part in the village bank robbery here, they were wanted men and needed to be arrested.

Winston Stirwell, couldn't believe what he was hearing and seeing. Dollar signs flashed before his eyes as he thought a story was about to fall into his lap. "Ye ha, I knew I was right. They've come for the drivers. Where are the children Gwendoline?"

Oh yes, Gwendoline knew where the children were but although she wanted her husband to reap a good story she didn't want the police to frighten the children or drivers and drive them underground before the Intelligent Officer from her UFO Unit had time to arrive and arrest them.

"Winston, if you need to find the children you will have to put skis on. They could be anywhere".

"No you put your skis back on and look for them. Meanwhile, I'm going to stick to Inspector Moody".

Winston Stirwell did just that. He followed Inspector Moody into Santa's Grotto and became a little puzzled when he heard him ask for the elves Ernest Pratt and Alfred Pike. The temporary Santa and the elves on duty said that they hadn't returned back on duty yet. They had been seen out on the slopes giving some skiing lessons and should have been back about ten minutes ago.

"Oh great" huffed Inspector Moody "I knew we shouldn't have put the sirens on. If they've heard us they will never come back".

"What do you want those two for officer?" barged in Winston, holding a hand sized tape recorder in front of the officer to show he was on official business.

"Sir, if I find you under my feet once more I'll ……"

"Inspector, they've have been seen on the slopes, just recently", butted in one of his officers.

"Well, you had better get some jet skis".

So off went four jet skis with Inspector Moody in the lead and his two officers following and not forgetting Winston Stirwell the freelance reporter at the rear. They had no idea where they were going so they drove here there and everywhere. Where ever they saw a group of skiers that's where they went.

Meanwhile, the two off duty elves were dashing around the slopes trying to shake of Snow. They thought if they could just get back to the village cottage, they could collect the wooden box marked [sewing machine] that they had originally been contracted to steal from David Seymour. They could place it in his Ford Popular and make a getaway back to where they came from.

Snow was determined however not to lose them but suddenly realizing she was lost and remembering her promise to Beth, to call her if in trouble, she pressed the buttons on her wrist Vigil.

Snow could see the elves ahead and that they were skiing towards a sharp cliff edge.

"Ernie we have to turn"

"No, we've jumped before"

"Yes but the little one hasn't" argued Alfie hesitantly as he looked back at the little child who was determined not to let her present go.

The cliff edge came very quickly after that and Ernie and Alfie disappeared over it.

"If they can do it, then so can I" thought Snow.

Snow bent her knees and got ready for the leap.

"No Snow" screamed Beth, Luke, Tayla, Jimmy and George as they pounced on her just a metre from the cliff edge.

"They've got my present!" cried Snow, trying to free herself and get a glimpse over the edge.

"It's not worth it Snow. What if you got hurt" urged Jimmy and George simultaneously putting their arms around her to pull her back.

The Viriddion visitors stood at the cliff edge for a little while in silence as they tried to get their breath back. They knew they needed to get back before the light began to fail but couldn't resist one last glimpse over the cliff edge for the elves.

They looked… and what they saw before them was…

… The Logan brothers in their black helicopter rising to the top of the cliff edge with the two elves wiggling and shouting in a net hanging below the helicopter.

Sounds of "Ye Ha, Hurray and clapping" exploded from the Viriddion visitors.

Brandon opened his portal and shouted, "See you back in the village".

As Beth, Luke and the children skied slowly back to

the main slopes, they could hear several ski jets above them going in and out of the trees. When they arrived back at the reception area they were met with Gwendoline looking a little worried.

"Oh there you all are. Gosh you do look tired. I thought you may have disappeared.... I mean I thought you may have gone home before I could say good bye".

"We've just been for a long ski. We're going back to the village now", replied Beth smiling at Snow.

SIXTY-THREE

FLASHING LIGHTS AND BLARING SIRENS

Inspector Moody, his officers and Winston were still on the hunt for the two off duty elves. The light was failing and they were all getting a little argumentative with each other, as to which direction they should be going in, when Inspector Moody's mobile went off. It was the station informing him to come back because two men had handed themselves in.

"What do you mean, handed themselves in!"

"Well, they're not exactly in. They're still outside. Best you come and see for yourself".

Inspector Moody turned the team around and made his way back to Santa's grotto, collected the cars and rushed back to the station with all lights flashing and sirens blaring.

Winston Stirwell desperately wanted to jump in the police car with them but, by the look on Inspector Moody's face, he wasn't even going to go there, so he had to make do with running back to the village with his wife.

"Winston love, I don't understand, what's the hurry?"

"Two men have handed themselves in. I bet it's those drivers. The pressures got too much for them, transporting those kids around, although it could be the two other strange men. Well, either way, this is my story", as he quickly got his camera out ready for some pictures.

When Inspector Moody and his men finally reached the village they were met with a large crowd of children and their parents chanting "Set Santa Free". This was not unusual because the demonstration by the children had been building up over the past few days but, the village was now packed with chanting and crying children.

As Inspector Moody and his men made their way through the crowd, dodging the odd snow missile, they were brought to a sudden halt by a couple of very angry men dressed as elves, entangled in a large net. The net had a note fixed to it which read: "The bag in our hands contains the money we stole from the village bank" and it was signed: Ernest Pratt and Alfred Pike.

By the time Winston and Gwendoline had pushed through the crowd, Inspector Moody and his men had dragged the net along with two screaming elves into the station and locked the doors.

Beth, Luke and the children couldn't see the Logan brothers anywhere so they waited excitedly outside the model shop, which had pleased the twins no end, whilst joining in with the odd chant "Set Santa Free".

Complete darkness had now fallen over the Lapland village and the lights in shop windows and Christmas tree outside the police station seemed even more sparkly because it was the night before Christmas.

Snowflakes were beginning to fall softly again when the police station door opened and Santa appeared, followed by two young men.

The children erupted with cheers and laughter. Beth, Luke and the Viriddion children watched on in delight as the village children filed past their Santa giving him a big hug and the parents giving the Logan brothers the occasional pat on the back.

Winston, of course, got his picture although the Officers continued to refuse him entry into the station for the story, much to his annoyance of course. His wife Gwendoline, however, appeared to look on proudly at the two young men who had obviously played a part in releasing Santa on Christmas Eve.

As the village children and their families slowly made their way home, Santa walked back to the log cabin with the Viriddion visitors. He constantly looked around him to see if he was being followed because the last thing he wanted was the Viriddion visitors to be caught up in the drama of a criminal gang selling illegal animal fur.

SIXTY-FOUR

CAPTAIN GENESIS

Back on Viridis 6000, Captain Genesis and his young crew were in trouble. The atmospherics were faulty and playing up and it had been reported to him from young Nathan in engineering, that unless they leave planet Earth or take the ship to the surface within the next twelve hours, they would all die of suffocation.

Roger Baker and daughter Sarah from intelligence were also now visiting the bridge and informing Captain Genesis that, the American UFO Unit was sending over an Intelligence Officer to arrest the children in Lapland. From what he could gather, Officer Gwendoline Stirwell-Twine had befriended them, to keep an eye on them until he gets there.

"Is there any way we can get a message to Beth" pleaded Captain Genesis.

"Any contact from us or from them to us, as you know Captain, will pin-point our position to anyone who may be looking for us".

"But, if we're going to have to leave within twelve hours, one way or the other, what have we got to loose".

"I suppose we could risk a contact with Rubin McDonald in Scotland. When the children called upon him on their way to Lapland, he would have given them a mobile to keep in contact with them. But, if our contact is traced to Rubin, we could be putting him at risk!"

"We haven't got a choice - just one call. Meanwhile, I'll get a decision from the rest of the crew as to what they want me to do. To leave Viridis 6000 or take it to the surface; the decision cannot wait for the children to come back. If we leave Earth, we will have to leave the children until we return. If we take the ship to the surface, it might give the children a chance to get back before we leave ......"

"...or get caught" chipped in Louis, who although only fourteen years old was beginning to catch on to the reality of landing on Earth. "Why can't they have a special landing area for visiting space ships, it would solve a lot of problems!"

"Yes, if only things were as simple as that" smiled Old Ridoros as he entered the bridge and hearing the suggestion by Louis. "Captain another thing we need to think about is, how are we going to stop the Yapikus visiting Earth?

"Hmm, I agree but I was hoping the children might be part of the plan but we will need time, which I fear is running out for us".

As Roger and Sarah left the bridge, Captain Genesis caught Sarah trying to make friendly eye contact with him, which he so wanted to acknowledge but, how could he think about his personal relationship in the situation they were now in. He needed to keep focused.

SIXTY-FIVE

DAVID SEYMOUR MEETS VIRIDDION VISITORS

In the Lapland log cabin, Beth had run a bath and prepared a meal for David Seymour, the newly released Santa. After his bath and a good meal he spent time talking to the Viriddions. He learnt how many of the older Viriddions' had died on the journey to Earth and how his son Michael and his wife were two of them.

When he first learnt this news, he became very silent and began to wonder what life was all about and, what his purpose in life was now, but when they introduced Snow to him as his Granddaughter, it all became very clear.

It became clear why this little one had asked for the return of her mother and he held her on his lap for a long time.

The children had the opportunity to tell David Seymour about the Yapikus visits and how they had managed to vaccinate only a few animals.

David was able to tell them about the lady he had seen wearing a multi-fur coat that could only have been manufactured by the Yapikus and how he found the man who was selling them.

He continued to explain how Pratt and Pike had sought him out for work and then took over his cottage and about the two strange men who had been watching his cottage, even whilst in custody

The Viriddion visitors could clearly see how and why David Seymour had stopped contacting Viridis but they didn't want him left in that situation, so they suggested that he keep Brandon's mobile. That way he could keep in touch with Rubin McDonald the E-Contact in Scotland, as Liam and Brandon felt that he could be trusted.

Time was getting on and the Viriddion visitors could hear children voices outside the log cabin and it became clear to them that the village children were getting anxious about Santa not being back in his grotto for the delivery of his presents that night.

"Yes, and that Winston guy is out there again. Oh, it's serious, he's got his wife with him this time", smiled Brandon "He doesn't give up, does he? What does he want now?"

"Well, if he's about to do his night spying let's give him something to watch. Beth, we're ready to leave, aren't we", asked Liam.

With a nod from Beth, he suggested that, whilst the carrier was still in the garage, everyone should get in the back, including Brandon, and to keep their heads down. He told Santa to leave by the front door and shout "Good bye, see you later" before closing the door and meanwhile he would drive the carrier out, leaving the garage open, as if he was about to return and he would also leave the light on in the log cabin, so Winston would think he was watching a full cabin, except, Liam who he thought might be returning later.

All went to plan and Santa waved to the village children, telling them that he was just getting a lift back to the grotto, as he climbed into the front seat with Liam.

As they slowly drove through the Lapland village for the last time David Seymour suddenly asked them to stop because he had forgotten something he needed to take to the grotto. He ran into a cottage not far from his and after a short while he came out with a box.

Just as he was getting back into the carrier a very official looking black and white car that seem to be in a hurry passed them and Liam could see in his side mirror that it had stopped outside their cabin and Winston and Gwendoline had got out of their car to meet it.

"Strange", he thought.

When they got to the grotto they let Santa and Snow out. Snow gave her Granddad a great big hug and he apologised for the present. But, Snow said "it was the best present ever because it had set her Granddad free!"

"Even so" said Santa "This is your real present Snow. I'm sorry I didn't get a chance to wrap it in pretty paper".

Snow excitedly opened the box, which had Bertie written on it. She gently took the white, beige and black fluffy ball in her arms saying "Hello Bertie". Bertie opened his eyes and licked her on the cheek; he was not going to pretend to be asleep this time.

"Thank you. Thank You Granddad", said Snow hugging her Granddad and squashing Bertie in the middle.

Then Snow, with Bertie in her arms, ran off to the carrier which Liam and Brandon had quickly transformed into a helicopter and they were off.

As Santa waved to the Viriddion visitors, tears began to roll down his face, as he thought "It was nice to meet you Snow and I hope to see you again soon".

THE END

GLOSSARY

(In order of book appearance)

Captain Robert Genesis – Captain of the Viridis 6000 (Grandson of Old Ridoros)

Old Ridoros – (Earth Great Grandfather of Robert, Elizabeth and Julie Genesis)

Elizabeth Genesis – Known as "Beth" Head Teacher in Animal Communication Inter-actionism Unit on Viridis 6000 (Granddaughter of Old Ridoros and sister to Captain Genesis

Luke Montgomery – Teacher of Animal Communication & Inter-action on Viridis 6000 (Nephew of America E-Contact).

Tayla Winsor – 14 yr old Viriddion visitor

Jimmy and George Penn – 12 yr old twins

Snow Seymour – 6 yr old Viriddion visitor.

Louis – Bridge Technologist

Nathan – From Maintenance Unit

Roger Baker – Officer of Intelligence Unit on Viridis 6000

Sarah Baker – Daughter of Roger Baker

Rubin McDonald – A Viridis Earth Contact.

James Logan – A Viridis Earth Contact (Earth Grandfather of Liam and Brandon)

Joseph Montgomery – American E-Contact trained Aviator (Uncle of Luke Montgomery)

David Seymour – A Viridis Earth Contact.

Gwendoline Twine – Officer in American UFO Unit.

Winston Stirwell – Freelance Journalist

Earnest Pratt – Large Elf

Alfred Pike – Little Elf

Inspector Moody – Inspector of Lapland Village Police Station

Julie Genesis – Younger sister of Robert and Elizabeth.

Lemmie – Looks like a type of slender Loris (Brought from Planet Viridis by Snow's Mother)

Mikey Montgomery – Student Pilot (Younger brother of Luke Montgomery)

Rachel – Zoo Game Keeper

Bertie – Siberian Husky Pup

The Sub-Marina/Astrophysics and Aviation Academy – Viridian's who have studied and passed vigorous examinations in the study of power-dynamic machinery for travelling under water, on land, above the land and in space.

The Terrestrial Threats to Animal Life Foundation - Viriddions who have studied and passed vigorous examinations in the study of Terrestrial Threats to Animal Life.

The Distinguish College of Animal Communication and Inter-actionism – Viriddions who have studied and passed vigorous examinations in the study of animal communication.

Viridis Multi-Transporter – A vehicle that can be transformed into a submarine, car, helicopter or boat.

Earth Contact – An E-Contact. An Earth person who has spent time studying on Planet Viridis and who has returned to Earth to pass on their knowledge in their employed positions on Earth and to continue to provide a safe house for Viriddion visitors.

Lightning Source UK Ltd.
Milton Keynes UK
174090UK00001B/7/P